I0763530

# *HAVEN'S LEGACY*

**OTHER TITLES BY THE THIS AUTHOR**

Search for Haven
Bibix
Tales from the Kodiak Starport
Crisis at the Kodiak Starport
Showdown at the Kodiak Starport

# *HAVEN'S LEGACY*

***JUSTIN OLDHAM***

**SHADOW FUSION LLC**
**ANCHORAGE**

Published in the United States of America by Shadow Fusion LLC
http://www.shadowfusionbooks.com

Library of Congress Control Number: 2019900070

ISBN: 978-1-935964-66-7

*For unremembered thousands who slowed the Collapse,*
*anyone among us who has brought light into darkness,*
*and those who quietly build for the future without praise.*

# PROLOGUE

2050-2100 (*B.C.: BEFORE COLLAPSE®*) is remembered in books and movies as a Second Renaissance. Bio-engineering sciences repaired polluted ecosystems, banishing most infirmities and disease from humans. Whole species of plants, animals, and marine life were "improved" to ensure their long-term survival.

Advancement sparked a sense of worldwide optimism. Consumers and politicians began to rethink the future as Artificial Intelligence (AI) introduced new forms of recreation and employment for restless billions who would never have to work if they didn't want to.

Legal scholars regarded manmade technology as the property of its inventors or owners until it became a public domain resource. Humanists argued in favor of limiting AI sentience, hoping to prevent technological dependence. Transhumanists insisted that self-sustaining infrastructure and impartial judiciaries administered by incorruptible AIs would allow Humanity to flourish.

Humans for and against self-aware technology pursued their agendas publicly and privately. Terrorism of every kind masqueraded as AI threats of all sorts, which did include AI emancipation by force. That's why rogue AIs weren't the only cause of the Collapse, though they were a substantial contributing factor.

We're not sure when Artificial Intelligence got loose. It seems to have become uncontrolled just a few years before the 22nd Century. Explorers still find evidence of efforts to slow the decline. Sometimes, we are able to figure out who they were and what they might've done. As you know, the passage of time erases useful clues. Many mysteries remain unsolved.

* * *

2100-2150 (*D.C.: DURING COLLAPSE®*) is confusing, if you rely on games, books, and movies. Activism and terrorism blended, blurred, and merged to become a sinister force far worse than anyone had ever seen before.

Political corruption and corporate greed were no match for the multifaceted forms of friction that ate governments and corporations faster than they could assess what was happening to them.

Loss of civic freedoms did little to slow the spread of hostile AIs. Socioeconomic extremists colluded with eco-terrorists in escalating efforts to make their demands more widely known and enforced. Fragmentary proof suggests that early migrations from cities, metroplexes, and some arcologies began as technophobic reactions to AI-inspired sympathizers and their militant tactics.

They weren't all refugees. Some of the early founders who established fortified enclaves were well-funded leaders of social movements. Many of those places exist today as thriving post-Collapse villages and towns.

When fighting in highly automated cities displaced millions of traumatized people, the dispossessed were directed by dwindling armies over choked roads to government-sponsored relief camps or to better-equipped relocation centers known as Haven Sites. Others made their way enclaves that would have them.

National governments ceased to exist after 2150. This period is now referred to as *A.C.: AFTER COLLAPSE®*.

There appears to be some confusion about what it was…or is. It's nothing more than a good story in some parts of the post-Collapse world. For people who have nothing to lose, the idea of Haven may be just enough to give them hope when they need it most.

# CHAPTER ONE

July 2200 (A.C. 50, five decades after the Collapse) - Warm summer rain fell on a ramshackle orphanage located near what had been Fort Dent, Washington. Sixteen year-old Alexander held court on the porch, surrounded by younger kids. Shaggy, uncut hair and mismatched glasses lenses in bent wire frames made him appear demented.

"Preacher says there is no Haven," nine-year old Tasha related calmly.

"It's real," Lex insisted.

"How d'you know?" she challenged.

This was his favorite part of the game. He looked around to be sure they were alone.

Lex lowered his shaggy head and his voice deepened. "My parents were soldiers on their way to Haven with important people. They were ambushed by machines. It happened a little north of here, a bit closer to the city. Ten years ago, when I was no bigger than you are now!"

The small brunette was a newcomer who'd spent several years foraging on her own. She glanced around with a sour face. "Preacher says anyone who looks for Haven is wasting their time. It's a miff. Supposed to make you happy because, you know..."

Lex pulled a wrinkle out of his dirty white T-shirt while the gaggle felt silent. Nobody joked about parents they'd lost or been separated from. "Haven is no *myth*," he insisted. "People pass through here two or three times a year, on their way. They can't all be wrong."

"C'mon Lex," somebody complained behind him. "Who cares if it's real or not? Not like we can go there. Get to the goodies so we can finish chores before lunch!"

The boy's eagerness to end the game was understandable. All of them wanted a share of the loot Lex always brought back from the suburbs of Seattle that were only visible as a long, dark line on the northern horizon.

Lex enjoyed his recurring role just a little too much. "Haven is much different. This place is named for that forest over there." He pointed east. "All those trees were on the other side of that highway. You can only see parts of it now. Something really fierce must have happened to wreck that road."

All eyes followed his every move. "Rock Park has two hundred adults in it. Not sure how many children. Haven has thousands of adults, or more. They grow lots of food and they've got all the clean water you'd want. They don't treat their orphans like salvage, either."

"But how do you *know*?" skeptical Tasha demanded when nobody else spoke.

"I still remember my parents," he declared solemnly.

"What if they lied?" she countered.

Most of the children who could recall anything about their parents at all tended to hold them in high regard. Preacher warned against idealizing or worshiping ghosts, but that didn't prevent Lex and others like him from cherishing their memories.

"They died protecting me," he explained assertively.

Tommy was a gaunt boy of ten with more patience than Lex had possessed at his age. Common knowledge was that his father had been a soldier. History lessons bored him. He interrupted Tasha's interrogation of Lex by sharply elbowing his way through the crowd, kicking a green rucksack on the floor near the teenager's feet.

"Stop telling baby stories and just give out the loot!"

The outburst made everyone be quiet.

Lex's mood remained sanguine. He reached into pockets on his patched jeans for handfuls of hard candy to quickly pass around. "I am looking out for you guys," he insisted while doling out each piece. "My folks taught me to scavenge. Someday, I'll show you how it's done."

Each child eagerly took the treats with greedy glee. They didn't care that every lump was crystallized solid, decades past any sell-by date.

When he'd given away all the candy, Lex bent over to adjust ragged sticky tabs on his muddy combat boots. He always did this to prolong the anticipation.

The cynical girl eyed him warily as he stood up.

"Look for yourself. People stop by the trading post once or twice a week. They buy food, camping stuff, and ammunition. Listen and you'll hear them talking about Haven before they go on. Funny thing is, they all seem to be going in different directions. Nobody can agree on where it is."

Everyone was too busy to argue. Tasha glared at him after a mighty swallow.

Lex silently watched them gnaw, chew, and crunch. He enjoyed the feeling he got from giving away some of what he'd found so close to the abandoned coastal city.

"Sometimes they have guns," Tommy chimed in.

"Who had guns?" Lex replied with phony ignorance.

"Them looking for Haven!" another child shouted, falling into the word trap.

Lex nodded. "Yeah, they usually have guns. Rifles and pistols. The kind of stuff we're not allowed to have inside the enclave. You don't see many energy weapons. I'm guessing it's because power packs are hard to find. When I ask about Haven, they give different answers."

None of them cared where Haven was, only that it could be. Leaving – going out on their own – was too scary to think of. Especially when free loot was at hand.

Tasha signaled defeat with lowered eyes. She laid a sly hand on Lex's pack in an effort to change the subject. "Preacher says you steal."

The timid accusation made him giggle. "Yeah, right. I steal from the dead. They don't really need it anymore. All that stuff is just lying around. Anyone can take it."

His logic appealed to her, though she was still intent on opposing his rule.

"What about the machines?"

Lex frowned and shook his head in her direction. "I've only seen one and it wasn't moving very fast. That was two years ago. Most of what you should worry about now is traps. They're everywhere, enough to make me sweat. There must be good loot far into the city. Only the bravest explorers go there."

Tommy sidestepped to punish Tasha for offending his leader with a sharp slap on her backside.

She whirled to growl at him.

The skinny boy kept a scarred fist up and ready. "C'mon, Lex. Give. Before Preacher gets back."

Lex wanted to ignore the scrap that was brewing. Tommy could take care of himself. All the orphans who were bold enough to spend time with him were assertive. It was their way of coping with prejudice and privations heaped on them by adults in the enclave who tolerated their presence. Preacher's constant moralizing seemed to make them feel good about what little food and shelter they provided.

"Lookout," Lex told Tommy while opening his bag.

Nobody else moved. They were too worried about being left out. Lex overlooked blatant signs of voracity and started unzipping the outer pockets on his pack.

Tommy pulled a static camouflage cap out of his back pocket and put it on. The military hat that had been his father's was too big for him. He wore it with pride. Anyone who had such keepsakes was fortunate.

Lex handed him a small, blue stuffed animal and a pair of protein bars. Tommy accepted what he was given and went to the edge of the porch where he could easily see the slim gate that Preacher would approach and open.

He kept his ears peeled just to be sure he wasn't missing anything good that might be going on behind his back.

Lex continued with the rest of his gift giving ritual. He had something for everyone. Nourishment was the most precious commodity to them. They gladly grabbed for the pre-packaged food he handed them.

Because most of them couldn't read, Lex named each item as he gave it away.

"Squeezy Cheese."

"Veggie Bits."

"Wonder Bars."

Preacher's legendary wrath was now a distant threat. Some ran inside the house to stash loot or eat unseen. Others ate the contraband where they stood.

Lex teased open the largest compartment in his pack before officiously revealing fat rolls of clean, white socks that he busily tossed in their direction.

Squeals of joy rippled through the jostling crowd as food-stained fingers fondled soft, warm, synthetic fibers. A few more kids ran off to spread prosperity or hide it.

Two children abruptly sat on the rough wood floor and pulled off their muddy, handmade leather shoes. They peeled off thin, crusty socks and laid them aside. Putting clean socks on over their dirty feet was a thrill, even though they were too big for them.

Lex observed everyone who remained on the porch with silent satisfaction. None of them knew about the better things he'd found. He never mentioned electronics or anything else that might tempt somebody to tail him.

"Better than Christmas!" an unseen child declared.

"Preacher!" Tommy called out when his keen eye saw movement that his distracted ears hadn't heard.

Everyone reacted when they heard the telltale sound of boots plodding through mud. All the orphans fled, leaving Lex surrounded by torn wrappers and dirty socks. He scrambled for the evidence as the gate creaked open.

Tommy melted away from his sentry position with a food-stained grin.

* * *

Preacher slopped his way through muddy puddles, crossing a bare patch of gravel-coated ground in front of his ramshackle house. Moisture fell in beads from his long, brown, leather coat and matching wide-brimmed hat. He paused in the rain to think.

He saw Lex moving around on the orphanage porch. He knew what was going on. Again. The aging android shook his white-haired head in mild frustration. So much to do and so little time. It was good for Lex to care about the welfare of his fellow orphans, even if he didn't appreciate their benefactor's methods.

Preacher looked up into the rain that tousled his hair. So many things that could've been fixed decades ago by willing humans were now beyond any hope of repair. Every major system in him would fail – soon.

"We're better than this," he mumbled, adjusting his hat with a gnarled hand. "You know that, don't you?"

He talked to himself without fear of being noticed, hoping that somebody heard his wireless transmission. He knew that the locals would forgive his eccentricity because everyone understood that preachers spoke to the Divine whenever they wanted to.

"*He's* better than this," Preacher declared to no one. "They all – okay, most – are going to do good things. I've been hard on them, so they'd learn. I can't tell them. They'd never believe me!"

The rusty gate rasped and groaned with a scraping sound that made him uncomfortable when he opened it. "Easy for you to say. I'm the one delivering bad news."

* * *

Lex cursed himself for being so slow. He snatched up one last piece of packaging and sat with the trash-filled rucksack in his lap.

Preacher shambled up the sagging steps and took off his damp hat to shake away the water. Tact was needed. "Good afternoon, Alexander. I'm glad you're back."

"Yes, sir," Lex acknowledged.

The old man made a show of noticing tiny scraps of shiny plastic under his feet. They littered the floor near Lex's chair. A part of him admired what Lex had done.

"It's bad enough that you're so quick to defy me when my back is turned. Must you be so sloppy in the commission of your crimes?"

The teenager smirked. "You'd get this stuff yourself if you could. I know that."

The elderly man grumbled and found his way into a nearby seat. "I do what I can without breaking the rules. You know that, too. Times are tough and people here are in no mood for your guff. What happens if –"

"I know the law."

Preacher leaned over to pick up a piece of litter. "That's not what it looks like."

Lex dropped his pack and stood. "The law says no powered equipment inside the walls without inspection and quarantine. Thirty days under lock and in the dark. All I bring back for them is food, clothes, and some toys. Okay, sometimes I scav tech. Those hypocrites on that high and mighty council you like so much pay big for what I sell them – after it's been okayed. Maybe you never noticed, but I sell mostly batteries and stuff you have to plug in before it works."

Preacher sighed while reminding himself to be calm. "I appreciate everything you've just said. That doesn't change the facts. Any designated by charter to be a child isn't allowed beyond the walls. They must stay inside to avoid harm. Especially kids without parents. They can lock you out if they wanted to."

"There are so many holes in those walls," Lex fumed. "Rats and roaches come and go with more freedom –"

"That's not the point!" Preacher snapped, "You sneak off for days at a time. Children aren't allowed to bring *anything* into the enclave. You, of all people, know why that rule is important!"

"I'm just as good at –"

Tactfulness wasn't working. The android raised his voice just a little more. "Only adults can bring in salvaged goods, *after* they have been quarantined and inspected at the outpost."

Lex took a step closer to Preacher. "I am *not* a kid!"

"Their law says you're not an adult."

Lex was about to swear.

Preacher stood with all the authority he could muster. "Alexander, please. I need you to be a better example. The law *is* uncompromising. All of this is their attempt to avoid past mistakes. I'm glad you can see beyond their technophobia. Someday, when you're in charge, you can change a lot more than you realize. Until we are sure there is no machine threat, we've got to be careful."

The younger man was unsatisfied. Some rules made sense, others didn't. "I haven't seen a moving machine in two years. How hard would it be to set up some gear to look for wireless signals? No! Can't, or won't."

"My point is that you've seen them!" Preacher protested, "By your own admission, you have seen them. That's enough for any restrictions to stay on the books."

Lex struggled to contain his emotions. "Tell them to feed us more and give us more clothes. I won't go back. I'll give my word."

Preacher was pleased to hear something more than anger from the tormented teen. "You're in no position to bargain when them. Demands only get you thrown out. I know you've seen that happen, too."

Lex pushed his makeshift glasses back up his nose. "Be patient, just don't do anything. You send too many mixed messages. You're nice, and then you make things rough on us. You can't seem to do anything when it really matters. Why won't you stand up to them? I do."

Preacher brooded for a moment, tugging his beard. "Yes. Well. Someday, when I'm gone, you'll get to see what it's like to ask these people for things they don't want to give."

"What makes you think I'm going to stick around?"

The old man laid his wet hat aside on the porch rail and paused before speaking. No more tact. "Alexander, I'm dying. The doctor confirms it. Now, just hold on a moment! It's not that bad. I've had a long life, and I've got time – just enough to help you take charge."

"No!"

"I was hoping—"

"Go to Hell!"

Preacher flinched. He folded his hands to display patience he didn't feel. "There will always be orphans, and they will always need somebody to care for them. Adults around here aren't what you consider generous. They might be. Someday, when there's more to share."

"Only if somebody points a gun at them."

Rain clattered down through flimsy gutters as they faced each other. Lex saw that he was slightly taller than Preacher. The realization made him take a closer look. Sad eyes and bushy eyebrows broadcast a silent plea. The old man was showing real signs of sincerity.

Preacher relented. "I have no taste for violence."

Lex giggled derisively.

The elderly fellow took a deep breath. "You're angry and your preference for aggression is understandable. Alexander, I'm trying to offer you another choice."

"Stop calling me that!"

Preacher conceded the grievance with a brief nod. "Channel your hostility into something more positive," he continued. "Please, take my place when the time comes. Do the right thing for these little ones. When you've earned their respect, everyone who matters will listen."

Fear made Lex's heart race. "Why me?"

Preacher frowned at Tasha, who dared to show herself through an open window. He waited until she was gone. "You've been packed and ready to leave for the last four years. I can't get that silly notion of Haven out of your head. And yet, you're still here. That tells me you care about what happens."

Lex was momentarily speechless. He'd come to expect lectures about his law breaking. He wasn't prepared for *this*. "I-I can't stay. I have to find Haven."

"Why?" Preacher demanded.

"My parents –"

Preacher suddenly lost his temper and grabbed Lex by the throat with one bony hand. His patience was gone. He shook Lex with a portion of his pent up fury.

"Your parents are dead!"

"Haven is real," Lex gagged.

"How many times do I have to tell you – all of you?" the outraged android spluttered. "The Haven Initiative was a relief program, not just one place; it was intended to help you when –"

Lex overcame his fear and grappled with Preacher. "Far. Hard to find," he choked while tearing free.

Preacher released his opponent, blushing with shame at the thought of accidentally killing him. In spite of his apparent age, he had more upper body strength than Lex would, even if he were more physically fit.

Lex recoiled with his own sense of embarrassment. The old man was out of control. He'd never seen him like this. Conflicting emotions made him feel sorry for what he'd said and done so hastily – and yet, still ready to knock the old goat's teeth out.

Preacher shook his hairy head in self-recrimination. "This isn't how I wanted to tell you. It's not how I wanted to ask you!"

Lex made a fist and dropped it.

"You're just so thoroughly single minded," Preacher scolded. "It's not always about you. There are bigger things at stake. Can't you see that?"

"You're dying?"

"Cancer," Preacher lied. Passing for human was good and bad in the post-Collapse world. Very few people were observant enough to figure out who or what was in their midst, including the manmade machines that had played their own part in the end of what had been.

Lex was incredulous. "Dying? As in –"

"Yes!" Preacher replied, waving his arms.

The young man was dazed. He sat. "I don't know what to say. Who'll takes care of us?"

Preacher took a deep breath. Noise inside the house told him they had a larger unseen audience.

"You will."

Lex showed signs of slow comprehension. His facial expression changed several times.

Preacher grasped his hat and sat quietly. "I'm sorry," he whispered.

Lex felt numb. He looked over Preacher's shoulder, at pairs of inquisitive eyes staring through cracks or gaps in the walls and open door. "Don't ever touch me like that again."

Preacher was remorseful. He stepped back and lowered his voice. "Alexander, I really am quite sorry. You don't always bring out the best in people."

"Neither do you."

"We are flawed men," Preacher concluded.

Lex's mind became sharp again.

"When does it happen?" he asked pointedly.

Preacher squirmed. "It's a matter of months."

"How exactly does Doc know?" Lex inquired.

The logical android relaxed before telling more lies. "I've been seeing Doc quite privately about my condition. He's been keeping an eye on me for quite some time now, and there is no doubt about what comes next."

Lex nodded without knowing what to say.

Preacher modulated his tone, attempting to be civil. "You have got to mend your ways with these people. We need time to make them accept that you are my replacement."

"I'm not a preacher," Lex managed to get out.

The fatigued android caressed his hat. "There's more than one kind of preacher."

"I don't want your job."

"All I can do is ask."

Lex visibly wrestled with his resentment.

Preacher forced himself to continue, in spite of Lex's obvious inner turmoil. "If they bury me at all, it will be in an unmarked grave. They'll throw the lot of you out. *All of you.* It's not right, but they *will* do it."

"Bastards."

"Watch your language," Preacher corrected.

"Why do they hate us so much?"

Preacher mumbled to himself pensively. He sat up. "The community doesn't hate you. They're just resentful about…things. It's not really their fault."

"What can they be so cranked about?" Lex griped.

Preacher bobbed his head. It was a good question, and a sign that Lex was paying attention. "Everybody dislikes something, even if they don't know they do it. Fear of the unknown is older than written history. Hunger, sickness, and general misery make people mad."

Lex looked around. He grabbed his stained pack. "What have they got to be jealous about?"

Preacher struggled within himself to find words. "Most of the adults in Rock Park are old enough to remember when this place was just abandoned houses. They're fighting hard to feed and clothe all their own kids. It bothers them to give up anything at all for children who aren't their own."

The answer wasn't nearly as sinister as Lex feared. A part of his maturing mind accepted it. His adolescent ego resisted while he searched for any excuse to refuse. "So much for that load they've been shoveling about fair shares for a fair day's work."

Preacher raised his hand. "I won't tell you again about that language!"

Lex dropped his pack. "You don't get to boss me anymore. Whack me again and I'll tear your head off."

Preacher shivered when he saw hateful fire blaze in the young man's eyes. It was just as intense as the rage that motivated men to fight machines for reasons that nobody remembered clearly. His heart sank when Lex grabbed his bag and stomped into the house.

Preacher unbuttoned his coat, knowing that he only had one more chance to reason with Lex. If he could not plead his case well enough, the enclave's orphans would be alone and out of luck.

# CHAPTER TWO

Lex woke early the next day after very little sleep. Growling in his stomach reminded him of his missed dinner. He sat on the edge of his plastic mattress before striking a match on the edge of a cracked dresser.

He lit the smoky wick on a stubby, tarnished oil lamp, blowing out the match before tossing it in a garbage can. Lex looked down at his bare feet as the light came up. All he could make out were a pair of fuzzy blobs.

He was significantly farsighted. He'd been that way since birth. As far as he knew, his parents never had a chance to correct the problem. Very few people in the enclave had such disorders. It was enough to make him feel different in an uncomfortable way.

Preacher warned that most people with low vision didn't last very long. Those with minor vision problems could get by if they were careful. Anyone else with worse eyesight usually died young because they couldn't see what was dangerous.

Lex yawned while running both hands through his long, greasy hair. His eyes adjusted to the bright light. He inspected his makeshift glasses. He used the corner of a sheet to clear smudges from both lenses before putting them on.

Like so many other things that were valuable to him, Lex had found his scratched spectacles near Seattle's ruins. He sported improvised eyewear in a spiteful effort to mislead the adults in Rock Park. He didn't want anyone to know where he could get better salvaged glasses from, any time he wanted them.

Lex thought about yesterday's unpleasant encounter with Preacher. The man was quite serious about dying. His request for Lex to take over as chief orphan wrangler seemed strange to the point of being unusual, even for such a taskmaster.

The teenager's first reaction had been white-hot rage. Comprehension came only after hours of simmering, followed by depression-induced sleep and dreams of entrapment and betrayal. Preacher didn't understand Haven because he had no connection to it.

The old man talked big about the power of empathy, going on and on about the importance of considering the other guy's point of view. It wasn't hard for Lex to figure out why anyone would want to find that place. Even if it wasn't real, something like it must be possible.

The worldwide Collapse that was so well-known to adults meant very little to him. It had opened old wounds in all societies that most everyone thought were healed. Old hatreds, that Preacher said should *not* be, were alive and well in the enclaves. Lex was able to wrap his brain around bigotry and hypocrisy when he bothered to look. The rest of it was harder to recognize and understand.

Thoughts of being in charge of *anything* in Rock Park made Lex feel uneasy because he feared having it all taken away. All he'd experienced in the last ten years suggested that power was corruptive and accountability was highly overrated. Never mind what Preacher said, scrawny kids like him lost out to stronger, smarter adults. Violence was the only thing they seemed to respect. Force could change their minds about anything!

Lex surveyed the dusty, peeling walls of his room. He and Preacher were the only ones who had their own. Everyone else was packed in wherever they fit.

Seeing the light fixture in the ceiling made him sigh. It hadn't worked since the regional power grid failed. "Years ago."

Lex stood and stretched through another yawn. Childhood terrors about the night of his parents' death added to his insomnia. His anger at Preacher had cooled during his tossing and turning, giving his subconscious mind a little time to consider his next move.

Muddy footprints on the floor led to combat boots that appeared to be waiting for him. He slid off the bed and pulled on his pants. It would be *so* easy to leave. They couldn't stop him. He went out through their walls often enough to do it in the dark without a flashlight.

Something about the nature of this new conundrum made him feel awkward. He was not really frustrated. He wasn't mad, nor did he feel insecure.

"What's wrong with you?" he asked his reflection. The face in the streaked mirror that looked back at him disapproved in the same quiet way Preacher often did.

Was he thinking seriously about staying to look out for the others? Lex laughed while reaching for his boots. He put them on quickly. Their snug fit was reassuring. That comfort made him reminisce about the other things he had that made him feel good.

He considered the loot he had stashed, miles away. Food and clothes were practical; he could give them away. The rest was electronics, forbidden inside the enclave. Getting caught with any of those gadgets, devices, or computers would mean being kicked out – or worse. Electronics of every sort gave him access to interactive books and learning tools that kept him busy for hours. He'd learned how to use them by trial and error when they didn't just talk to him.

Lex grinned wickedly when he thought about the few guns he'd found and practiced with. Preacher would flip if he knew about those.

Shelf-stable food he brought back to the orphanage did more than reduce hunger and make everyone grow. It improved everyone's outlook on life. They'd need him for that much if he was going to run the place.

His thoughts turned to what he could take to other enclaves in the region. It'd be traded for whatever Rock Park needed. Would that be enough to make the older folks like him?

"No," he decided out loud.

They'd have to be forced. That would mean more guns and other tools of war. He did have a few pistols and some body armor that was still too big for him tucked away in favorite hiding places, but that wouldn't be nearly enough to make the kind of changes he had in mind for this struggling town.

There were a lot of adults and they were well-armed. He'd need time to find better weapons than they had. Then he'd have to learn how to use them.

"How do you recruit an army?"

Glorious, intoxicating visions of what he might be capable of danced in his head. Revenge surged through his veins, more than enough to justify anything he'd do.

Dreams of using wealth and power to get what he wanted were not new to Lex, or any of the many strays who made their own way. That sort of thing had always been just out of reach for him. Until now.

Realizing his potential hit him like a jolt of electricity from an exposed wire. Preacher was willing to back him. That changed everything.

Perched on the edge of his unmade bed, the stark surroundings made one thing clear. He had limitations. Size and muscles did come with age. The rest would be guesswork. He needed Preacher's help to fill in the gaps.

Lex got up and put on a T-shirt that suited his mood – black fabric with short sleeves. Large, white print across the back and shoulders read *Security.* He shrugged into a torn static camouflage jacket, all thoughts of domination receding when he noticed a pile of his dirty laundry. Every piece of it would be stolen if he was gone too long.

Minor thefts like that never did genuinely bother him. That was the orphan way. Everybody took from everybody, in spite of what Preacher said about privacy and personal space. Nothing was "yours" unless you could defend it.

Lex spent the next five minutes quietly packing the few things he wanted to keep while his imagination went into high gear. A plan began to form, one that would allow him to cooperate with Preacher to take charge – after he came back with enough loot to bargain with.

He stood behind his bedroom door for two minutes, listening for any sounds in the hallway. None reached his ears. He went silently to the dresser and reached under it to remove a loose floorboard. Inside a small depression, he felt around for his ancestral artifact.

His fingers located the scuffed and scraped wireless phone that was a connection to his last vivid memory of both parents. A solar battery in the device was depleted. It hadn't been charged in years. Somehow, in spite of everything else he'd lost, he'd been able to keep it.

Holding the phone in one hand, Lex slowly sat on his bed. He hadn't allowed himself to think about the past in quite a while. Gunfire and explosions filled his ears as his imagination replayed the events of that desperate night like a movie he watched when he was alone.

* * *

They were hunkered down behind a burning SUV. Cool rain soaked them as flares fell out of the black sky, bathing the area with eerie, white, flickering brightness. Mom and Dad, in faded camo uniforms with helmets, were arguing. Something about being surrounded.

Six-year-old Lex got down on his hands and knees. He peered under the car to see mechanical feet stomping through grass and mud just a few yards way.

"Now or never!" his father insisted.

The child was so fascinated by what he could see that he didn't notice when his mother stooped to grab for him.

She scooped him up to eye level. "Lex, baby. We gotta go."

"Robots," he said, pointing.

Dad handed his wife a small, silver, wireless phone. "Clip this to his shirt. Auto dial should call Haven while the phone has a good charge. Somebody will come for you if they get the signal. Take Lex into the woods."

"Come with us!" Mom insisted while keeping an iron grip on Lex.

The unshaven man raised his grenade launcher in one hand to feed his last rocket propelled grenade into it. "Can't risk leading the machines to a populated area or Haven. I'll do what I can here, catch up to you later."

Mom wiped dirt off her son's face. "We could lead them away. Go in the opposite direction. It's still warm in the East. We'll have plenty of time to find shelter before the snow flies."

Dad turned to leave. He raised his launcher without warning to fire at a humanoid machine 30 yards away. The shaped charge slammed into the robot's torso. Contact detonators in the grenade set it off. A flash of scintillating red-orange light burned through its protective housing to melt vital components. Lex cried when small, hot pieces of the destroyed robot stung his arms and face.

His mother comforted him as smoldering fragments hit the ground. "See those woods? We're going in there. Lots of trees; no bots. Are you ready?"

* * *

Sixteen-year-old Lex opened his eyes and shook off the unwelcome recollection. A part of him still didn't want to relive what had happened next.

He glowered at his reflection in the dresser mirror. Familiar features stared back. He had his father's eyes and his mother's chin. Stubble on his jaw made him look older than he really was.

Lex took a deep breath and shoved the phone into a coat pocket. "I need some loot leverage with Preacher. He can't argue with me when I have something to trade."

Still thinking, he took one last look around before blowing out the lamp. "It'll be just my luck if he dies before I get back."

Lex slowly opened the door to his room and moved down the dim hallway. His boots crunched over grit on the bare wooden floor. No amount of grumbling from Preacher could keep the place clean.

Young ears picked up the sounds of his movement. Blankets and bedsprings stirred throughout the house. The others were used to Lex's eccentric behavior. Everyone except Preacher, that is, who wouldn't be surprised by his absence.

Lex paused in front of a door that was ajar. Tommy gently opened it, stepping swiftly into the shadows. He was fully clothed, with new socks on his feet.

"Heading out," Lex whispered.

"Yes, sir," Tommy nodded.

Lex took a sheathed combat knife out of his coat. "You know the drill. Anything happens while I'm gone, and you take the others to our safe place."

"Yes, sir," Tommy affirmed as he took the blade.

* * *

Preacher was waiting for Lex in the trampled yard just as he stepped off the porch. He was dressed against the morning chill in his customary brown hat and coat. One hand gripped a solid oak cane that was sometimes used for more than walking.

"Is this goodbye?"

Lex walked around scattered outdoor furniture before getting close to Preacher.

"You thought I'd bug out?" he accused.

"The possibility had occurred to me."

Lex shouldered his pack. "I probably should leave you guys to twist in the wind, but I won't."

"What changed your mind?" Preacher asked.

Lex looked back at the house. "Hey, they're just kids. It isn't right. We don't deserve to be treated like we've done something wrong. Our only crime is being alive. I'll have more of this worked out when I get back."

The old man sized up his future protégé. "That's got to be the first manly thing I've heard you say. Are you off to think or to find more food?"

"Why can't it be both?"

Preacher didn't challenge his obstinacy.

Lex noticed the leeway, brushing at his coat sleeve. "You said cancer. Last year, I found some cancer meds. They're in some kind of clinic. I'll dig them up, and a few other things. With any luck, it'll be what you need."

"Why so generous?"

The younger man nudged Preacher's wooden cane with the muddy toe of his boot. "Because you'll owe me. That'll make some of the changes I want easier."

Preacher shuffled to hide his outward discomfort. Lex's intentions could uncover things he shouldn't know. Fear of being discovered, in spite of his own pro-human attitudes, worried the old android.

"What about Haven?" he probed.

The optimist slumped. "First, make things better here. Then go."

Preacher put a reassuring hand on Lex's shoulder. "Alexander, please. You're just one person. You can't save the world and you can't keep me from the grave."

Lex bristled. Preacher said "person" when he would've said "man" to anyone else. "I can't save the whole world, but I *can* improve this little piece of it."

Preacher didn't speak. He had seen far too many tragedies in his long life, or been responsible for them. He wasn't concerned about the fate of his physical body. That part of humanity's shared past could only be banished by the passage of time. Knowledge of the conflicts that brought man and machine to the brink of extinction had to be lost or forgotten – if that was actually possible.

Lex walked away, around the house, toward the back yard and the gate that he preferred. He raised his voice. "I'll be back in three days with your meds and loot. There are few other things we should have around here."

"No guns!"

Lex refused to answer, making his way around piles of firewood, an obstacle course of trash cans, and toys. He opened the rickety rear gate and paused.

Preacher appeared suddenly behind him, as expected. "I mean that, Alexander! No guns. You'll never change anything if you always resort to violence."

Lex turned, speaking in a manner and tone that was an obvious imitation of Preacher. "One more thing. There will be no more 'Alexander'. My name is Lex. Break that rule and I *will* hurt you."

Preacher ignored the mocking. He watched Lex go without another word. There would be time to teach him better diplomacy. Later, when he was willing to learn.

Lex went out through the gate and through a hedge. He vanished with agility and speed.

Preacher turned back to the rundown house, instantly aware that spying eyes watched his every move from windows and through holes in the walls. Each step closer to the building made it easier for him to see darting faces. They were plotting. He'd have to put a stop to their mischief before breakfast or he'd have no peace until Lex returned.

## CHAPTER THREE

Lex moved fast over familiar ground, making his way down side streets and alleyways to avoid the enclave's roaming patrols. What had once been a recreational park with historic structures was now a growing community protected by semi-fortified ramparts with enough holes for any enterprising teenager to find his way through.

A combination of full-time police and volunteers enforced the after-dark curfew that kept residents indoors. What they lacked in manpower was made up for by handheld radios and a growing grid of streetlights that illuminated important areas inside the walls of the pre-Collapse subdivision. Clouds parted and the sky brightened. Residents of the enclave were shaking off their slumber in preparation for another long work day.

The smells of cooking food wafting from the homes he passed made Lex hungry. Dodging cops on his way out always gave him an adrenaline rush. He passed by dozens of houses with patchy lawns and small gardens. Wealthier people had electric cars in various states of repair parked on gravel driveways.

Like many other settlements in the region, Rock Park was built with improvised watch towers at odd intervals that were tall enough for outsiders to see. They provided an illusion of security.

Lex knew better. He'd passed between them without being noticed by bored pairs of sentries more times than he could count. He'd only ever been caught and detained by them once, nine years ago.

The locals knew he came and went as he pleased. Anyone who bought what he handed over for quarantine couldn't say very much about his comings and goings. They tended to ignore him in public – when they could.

Lex tried not to think about past slights as he passed between two noisy homes filled with his best customers. He waited for a slow-moving police cruiser to roll by before slipping into a storm drain. He shoved his pack through the steel bars that were meant to block debris. Wiggling through was getting harder as he got older.

The crawl in pre-dawn darkness was painful. He hit his head and tore his coat on sharp metal he couldn't see. Lex stood in what he knew to be a blind spot for sentries in the towers nearby. The shallow depression was thick with weeds and ankle-deep in mud.

He took a solar-powered flashlight out of his pack and flicked it on. Its weak beam showed him enough to avoid any more injuries. Past experience taught him that it was unwise to use a stronger light because it would attract predators of every kind.

Lex put on his pack and walked slowly down the length of a large concrete pipe covered by mounds of rusted metal and cement wreckage. He estimated the prefabricated tube to be 16 feet in diameter – more than enough room for his needs, even as an adult.

His muddy feet crunched through old trash. Most of it was his own leavings. The rest dated back to refugees who had fled from Seattle during the Collapse.

His skin crawled at the ghastly thought of treading on what could be the remains of men, women, and children whose lives might've been cut short by technical terrors that still invaded the nightmares of post-Collapse people.

The future hadn't mattered quite so much to Lex until two years ago. His run-in with a roaming robot near the ruins of Skyway rekindled fears of technology from his childhood.

He didn't know what kind of robot he had seen or if it had seen him. He shivered at the memory of hiding in the nearby forest for seven days, just to be sure he wouldn't lead that thing back to Rock Park. Nobody would've forgiven him for *that.*

He now pondered the nature and origin of that machine menace every time he snuck out of town. Nobody talked about "them" without some prodding. Subjects like that were off limits for reasons unknown.

A few of the tech savvy adults had claimed that the smarter machines could repair and rearm themselves. Lex marveled at that. Who in their right mind would build such a thing that could turn on them?

A worsening stink in the sewer pipe forced him to focus on the task at hand. He trudged on slowly for another ten minutes before seeing daylight.

Graffiti on the walls remained as a grim testament to the past. Peeling paint badly spelled out slogans like *Beat the Machines.* Names and dates were etched into the crumbling walls. Lex tried not to read them.

Climbing up through a jumbled maze of broken concrete brought him out into a shattered intersection that was densely overgrown with vines and other vegetation. He turned off his light and put it away before feeling his way around a burned out car.

Stepping away from the rear of the wreck, he found his way out of the maze. Caution made him slow down as solar radiance began to peek over the eastern horizon. His head swiveled from side to side while he listened for the sound of voices, hooves, booted feet, or auto engines. Tweeting birds and wind-rustled grass suggested that he was alone.

The elders who controlled Rock Park never denied rumors that their militia hid land mines outside the walls. Lex looked for the simple markings he'd left on trees to show a safe path through tall grass and around stumps.

He moved quickly between rows of tilled earth to pass through farming plots that the enclave claimed as part of its territory. Finding what was left of Interstate Highway 100 wasn't too difficult at such an early hour of the day. The remains of the north-south road would be busy enough to avoid by midday.

He maintained his slow, steady pace for three hours, careful to avoid the open fields where outlying farmers and ranchers would be already be hard at work. There was no point in being seen if he could help it.

The occasional sound of a tractor or a barking dog put him on edge. Passing through indy lands was never as easy as travelers made it sound when they gossiped at the trading post outside of Rock Park. Homesteaders were fiercely independent. They didn't take in strays or tolerate trespassers. Lex hoped silently to change their minds about that someday, now that he was planning for a better future.

There was just one more obstacle to overcome before he was beyond the reach of Rock Park. Two hours later, as the sun reached high noon, Lex gradually turned north and slowed his pace. He slithered through several bushes to reach one of his preferred vantage points.

A derelict police station stood empty at the outermost edge of what the rulers of Rock Park called their "turf." Nestled among a dozen rundown structures, the moldy precinct building was used by the enclave's militia to wait out the region's constant rain.

Lex crept up on the site when he was sure there was no one inside. Empty holes in the roof's exterior gaped like open wounds where solar panels had been removed for use in Rock Park. He often enjoyed poking around the place to see what members of the militia left behind. Most of what he found was food or home-brewed alcohol. Bread, blankets, and dried meat were sometimes stashed there, along with pieces of local cheese.

When he was younger, Lex enjoyed brazenly taking those things, knowing that somebody would go hungry. Now, he left them alone. Every now and then he'd find magazines for firearms, caseless ammunition, or portable memory archives containing pornography. He always took the porn, careful to leave the bullets for any defenders who might be unlucky enough to need them.

Satisfied that he was alone, for the moment, Lex got to his feet and went inside. Broken glass and plastic crunched under his boots as he entered through a transparent side door. Its lock had been broken years before he was born.

Lex made his way past a pair of smelly doorways that lead to defunct restrooms. He doubled back, just in case somebody had been careless enough to leave toilet paper in one of the stalls. No luck.

He crept deeper into the fire-damaged interior, past a large, pitted wall mural emblazoned with the motto *Protect and Serve*. Inner walls were lit by daylight streaming in through skylights made foggy by grit.

Lex halted when he realized something was different about the area he was in. Pulling out his flashlight and shining its beam, he probed the shadows in what had been a briefing room. Rows of rotting chairs faced a podium.

Tiny voices reached his ears. Lex shook his head, worried that he might be sick. Two steps to his left, nine steps forward, and three steps his right brought him within view of a wooden cabinet with a clear front. "This is new."

Lex cleared space on the floor near the new fixture to get a closer look. Kneeling in the gloom, his weak light revealed a large, black radio with a corded handset.

"Not something you see every day," he muttered.

The radio squawked, chirped, and mumbled to itself inside the handmade wooden box, behind a clear plastic door held in place by steel screws and aluminum hinges.

Lex was momentarily thrilled. "Look at that," he told his flashlight. "This thing is tapped into local power."

A thick, gray wire extended from the bottom of the cabinet and into the floor. He leaned in closer to listen, knowing he would hear Rock Park's radio chatter.

Male and female voices mingled through static.

"Tower Six, radio check. Still no sign of the second eastern patrol."

"East One, radio check. We're coming in for lunch."

"What *have* you seen today?"

"That kid with the glasses popped out this morning. He's long gone by now."

"Log it. We'll catch him someday."

Lex scuttled away from the radio. Embarrassment mingled with pride. "You won't catch me 'til I'm older than Preacher."

He eyeballed the powered radio with new interest. The plastic door was kept shut with a very small lock. Not the sort of thing to keep anyone out who really wanted to take that radio. "Just enough to keep the animals out."

Lex got up. The mysteries of the radio could wait. No telling when sentry would show up, and he had a mission to complete.

Thoughts of being caught energized him. He fled at a slow jog, determined to reach his favorite campsite before dark.

* * *

Lex trotted through unnamed ruins somewhere near what had been Skyway, approaching a major highway interchange. He stopped to relieve himself in a sprawling suburb. Drinking from a stained water bottle, he chewed gum or sucked on hard candy while walking over, around, and through one obstacle after another.

He'd learned long ago to go from one landmark to another, resting on any safe high ground that would allow him to see long distances. Rock Park was a speck on the horizon when the sun went down. Seattle's jagged skyline pointed upward into the night like fingers beckoning him to take risks.

* * *

Lex moved briskly, arriving at the wreck of a military airplane that was slumped on a rise within sight of several collapsed overpasses just after dark. The troop carrier had lift fans on all four sides that allowed it to fly. Its slate gray hull was always reassuring to touch. He opened a side hatch and crawled in.

Bones and rags littered the musty squad bay floor. Looters had stripped them and their vehicle quite clean decades ago. Lex pushed aside handfuls of spiderwebs and climbed up to the flight deck. Dozens of insects scurried to avoid his every step.

He used a screwdriver to open the damaged cockpit door before stepping in. A stiff breeze rocked the APC back and forth as he dropped into the copilot's chair.

"What's up?" Lex asked the dried husk that was still strapped into the pilot's chair.

Bugs crawled under the fabric of its dirty flight suit, through empty ribs. Lex recalled that it had taken many tries to open the warped cockpit door, which explained why the corpse hadn't been looted before.

Name tape on the soiled green flight suit read *Lewis*. Lex hadn't known if the pilot was a man or a woman until eight years ago, when he'd worked up the nerve to go through her pockets.

Based on what he found, Lieutenant Dorothy Lewis had been a U.S. Army pilot. Lex liked reading about pre-Collapse military matters. The system of ranks used by armies around the world fascinated him.

He rapped his knuckles impishly on her helmet. "Still not talking?"

Lex didn't know why it was fun to tease the dead. He pointed at the cracked and cloudy windshield, toward the city skyline in the distance.

"Has anything happened I should know about?"

Sections of the Seattle metroplex began to sparkle as the red glow of the setting sun reached their remaining glass and metal facades. Wartime pollutants in the air were still fading. Rumor had it that some old cities were still burning. Scholars believed it would take another hundred years for the skies to be clean.

Lex looked down at what was left of the lieutenant's bare feet. They'd fallen to pieces years ago. "Thanks for the boots. And everything else. I'm not sure when I'll be back. I've got new responsibilities and it's freaking me out."

He coughed. "I'll see if I can't lock or jam the door before I go. I know how hard it is to get privacy."

Lex wormed his way out of the cockpit and went to a cluster of equipment lockers in the back of the aircraft. He fumbled through the corpse's pockets in the dark until he found Lewis's desiccated thumb. Photovoltaic properties in the skin of the troop ship still provided enough power for some internal systems.

He pressed the thumb to a lock and it clicked open. Lex knew there was some kind of electronics implanted in that severed digit. Though he was unaware of it, his own vigorous bioelectric field powered the processor just enough to trigger the security device.

Lex recalled his father's explanation of such things. The little computer was some kind of personal identifier. It could store all sorts of information as data about someone. Bank accounts, medical records, criminal histories, and security access codes were just some of what one might contain for lifelong use.

"It's an ID chip," he recalled his mother saying.

The importance of such knowledge had been lost on Lex until he found Lewis and the lockable compartments inside the wreck. He opened one of them and took out the supplies he'd need for the evening.

Sleeping bag, pillows, and a big blue air mattress dropped to the floor. Floppy packets of food followed.

Lex located his one and only roll of toilet paper and went outside to relieve himself. He leaned on the airplane's warm flank, eating and drinking while planning.

The sight of so many ruins made him glum in spite of the fact that they also stimulated his imagination. Sometimes, he dreamed about what Seattle must have been like before the evacuations. The idea of so many people in one place, with many different jobs, was enough to make him curious about how it all had ended.

Moments like that made him think about the adults who shunned the place. How could they *not* go there? How could they ignore all those treasures? What would possibly make them stay away?

"Damned machines."

Lex had grown up on stories about vast robot armies capable of shaking the ground wherever they marched. Lack of knowledge and experience made him question the adults who seemed to relish telling those lurid tales.

"How does a bot survive without people to fix it?"

The question was just too big. He took his trash inside the wreck and barred the door. Something about the riddle suggested a need for cooperation, even if there was no trust.

"We might need them; they might need us."

Lex quit philosophizing. He inflated his air mattress and let it flop on the floor. A gentle wind began to blow as he lay down. It forced the grounded airframe to sway. It's back-and-forth motion always felt strangely soothing. He slept soundly with his clothes on.

# CHAPTER FOUR

Lex woke suddenly when the squad bay door rattled. The entire ship rocked back and forth as somebody outside tried to force their way in.

"Damn it!" a male voice shouted.

Lex leaped reflexively to his feet. His head bounced off the roof of low-ceilinged interior. He put a hand over his mouth to muffle the curse.

"Did you hear something?" a deeper masculine voice asked worriedly.

Outside, in the brisk morning air, three bearded men in mismatched clothing were investigating their find. One of them stood watch while the other two tried to find a way into the crumpled airframe. Pistols and knives hung from handmade vests alongside hand grenades.

Tig thumped slowly on the door with his large fist. "There better not be anybody in there!"

Jeremy was the only man present with a long gun. He held his light assault rifle in both arms, careful to stay away from the others.

"Look around, man. You see all these footprints? Lots of folks have been and gone."

Zeke pressed his shoulder into the stubborn door. "There's only a little bit of movement. I bet it's jammed. Might've happened when this thing crashed. We'll have to come back with sledgehammers or a cutting torch."

Tig gave up on the door. He ran around the plane to its furrowed front end. He jumped up on the broad nose and peered into the cockpit, through the windscreen. "Frag me! There's just one deader in there, strapped in. Crispy. I can see a helmet and lots of teeth."

Jeremy walked wide to get a better look at their prize. "That's a good sign. Looks like this beast hit pretty hard. Zeke is right. That door is bent."

Zeke climbed a strut, pulling himself up to the roof. "No turret, but I do see an escape hatch."

Tig bounded up over the cockpit onto the machine's broken back. He knelt next to the emergency exit to read large letters painted in yellow. "'W-warning, ex…ex-plo-sive bolts. Stand clear.' Does that mean it's trapped?"

"Hell if I know," Jeremy griped.

Zeke pulled himself closer. "See if you can kick it."

Lex started to panic when Tig jumped up and down on the hatch. The unstable VTOL began to shudder. Fear grabbed his guts and made his heart beat faster. Feeling his way across the dark compartment, he raised one hand to the roof, probing until he found the spot where the emergency escape hatch was.

"I got it!" Tig shouted.

Zeke cautiously scuttled away, ready to climb down. "Give it up, you idiot. That's not working."

Jeremy went to the squad bay door. "This can wait. We've got bigger fish to fry. Tig, come down!"

"Almost got it!" the marauder promised.

Lex gasped when he saw daylight blink through gaps in the hatch.

Zeke jumped from the wobbling wreck to the ground. "C'mon. This isn't getting us to Rock Park."

"Let 'em have Rock Park. We're gonna be rich!" Tig insisted, preparing himself for another bounce.

Jeremy had enough. "Get down here now, before I put a bullet in your butt. We're gonna hit Rock Park. Anyone who gets left behind gets left out."

Lex cringed at the mentions of the place he never could think of as "home." The implication was stunning. These men were part of a larger raiding force that was going to loot and pillage Rock Park. He swore quietly.

Sounds of breaking plastic and flecks of falling dust galvanized him into action. Instinct motivated him to reach for a short, wide, red handle on the overhead hatch to hold it shut. Loud explosions and a flash of light happened at the same time.

Lex fell to his knees, covering his head with an arm as the hatch – and Tig – were blown clear of the wreck by micro charges tucked in around the outer hatch seal. The blasts reverberated inside the hull, deafening Lex.

One of the old explosives was a dud. It didn't work. Inconsistent application of force caused the flying hatch to spin wildly. It sliced through Tig, cutting him in half. The marauder screamed in agony. His upper body landed yards away from the aircraft in a spray of blood. Each of his severed legs fell in separate bushes nearby.

Jeremy raised his rifle and swept the area. "Zeke!"

"On it!"

The experienced looter looked for nearby dangers. Tig *had* said something about explosive bolts.

"He's dead!" Zeke yelled near the legless corpse.

"Come on back!" Jeremy replied, waving his arms.

There was nothing to be done about this accident. The suburbs of Seattle were full of things that could take hands, eyes, or a life. Some threats were leftovers from the days when machines hunted humans. Others were just pre-Collapse tech, like this airplane.

Lex closed his eyes to avoid being blinded by daylight that was streaming in through a square hole in the roof. He reached for a folding seat and pulled it down to sit. He put on his glasses while the ringing in his ears faded.

Zeke found Tig's legs and stripped off their boots. He bent over the dead man to pick through his pockets. Tig's bad day was his good fortune.

Jeremy fumed when he saw what Zeke was doing. "It's gonna be like that, eh?"

Zeke was new to the clan. He didn't fully understand how things were done. A fair share meant fair treatment. No share meant that all bets were off.

Lex panicked when he heard sounds of movement. Scrapes and scratches moved up the side of the airplane. He fled to the cockpit and slipped inside. Leaving the door slightly ajar, he reached around the pilot to open the flap on her dusty shoulder holster.

"I'll bring this right back," he promised.

Lex didn't stop to think. He'd heard too many sordid tales about marauders and what they did to captured kids. Sweat beaded on his forehead, rolling down his neck as he took a ten round clip out of his coat pocket and loaded it into the nine millimeter semiautomatic handgun.

Jeremy landed in the squad bay with a hollow thud that made the ship bounce on its crushed landing gears. He stumbled on the air mattress and his feet became tangled in Lex's sleeping bag.

"Somebody's in here!"

Zeke was too focused on what he was doing to hear Jeremy's warning.

The rifle-toting man took his weapon off safety and looked around. Stale human body odor hung in the air. Discarded food wrappers littered the floor. The squad bay door was jammed with a piece of rusty iron. He eyed the cockpit and listened.

Silence.

"You might as well come out!" Jeremy shouted.

Lex held his breath and gripped his pistol.

Jeremy skulked over to the squad bay door, careful to keep the barrel of his rifle pointed at the cockpit door. He tried to pull the metal rod out of the door frame using one hand. It wouldn't budge.

He thought about the dead pilot. Just the sort of thing an explorer would leave alone if they were superstitious. It also might go untouched if there was no way to open that door.

Jeremy slipped a tiny flashlight off a loop on his belt. The thin, bright beam swept the interior, revealing open storage compartments and food packets on the floor.

"Don't make me come in there!" He bellowed.

Lex held his pistol firmly and flicked off the safety, just like his father had taught him.

Jeremy turned off his light and carefully put it away. One air mattress meant a single person – somebody who liked their comforts. There was too much lying around to be an accident. This had to be a scavenger's hideout.

He thought about calling for Zeke. There was more loot in here than he could carry. Might not be a bad idea to buy some good will.

The irritated man slung his rifle over one shoulder. Why share any of it? He gripped the scrap that jammed the door with both hands and pulled.

As Lex exhaled while using the toe of his boot to nudge the cockpit door open, he heard rasping metal.

Jeremy turned at the sound of a creaking rusty hinge.

Lex pulled the trigger twice when he could see his target. The pistol bucked in his hands. The reflex to aim came from practice, though Lex couldn't help thinking about the fact that he wasn't plinking at cans or cars. This was *real*. He was taking a life.

One of the projectiles missed and ricocheted around the compartment before embedding itself in a cabinet. The second slug struck Jeremy in the chest. He was dead before his twitching body hit the cluttered floor.

Zeke looked up from what he'd taken off Tig when he heard gunshots. "What now?"

No more shots. Drafts of wind blew sand in his face.

Zeke got to his feet. "You got trouble?"

No answer. He went to have another look at the loading door before climbing on the airplane.

"What's going on?"

He squinted to see a pair of booted feet in blue jeans on the floor inside the cargo compartment.

"Jeremy?"

Zeke lay flat and stuck his head inside. Jeremy was face down near the big sliding door. His rifle was slung. The cockpit door was halfway open. Food wrappers gleamed on the floor.

He sat up. Rising sun warmed his face. He thought. Somebody was in there with all that loot. Just one, probably out here alone. Nothing to stop Zeke from taking whatever he wanted, included Jeremy's rifle, *if* he could be smarter than the hiding scavenger.

He hopped down into the dark interior, hoping to take his opponent by surprise.

Lex forced himself to remain calm, tracking his target as he came into view. He fired three shots into Zeke.

The surprised man coughed and fell to his knees.

Lex bounded into the compartment with a growl, shooting the stunned man again. Zeke's head came off, spraying blood and bone all over the walls.

Lex's aggression was replaced by sudden revulsion. He gagged on his own rising bile, dropping his gun. Clawing at the iron bar that held it shut, he flung the large loading door open without any thought of what could be waiting for him outside.

The terrified teen threw himself from the vehicle, blinking through the glare of the rising sun as he sprawled on the hard ground. Disorientation made him queasy. His vision swam through tears of mixed emotion. More bile gorged his throat. The urge to throw up made his chest hurt.

He got to his knees, gulping air. The rush of hot, bitter stomach acid passed his lips in a torrent. He fell over onto his hands, spraying vomit.

Lex slowly recovered. Moving away from his mess, he sat upright, feeling shame. He'd certainly be dead if there had been any more of those marauders in the area. He cursed himself for his weakness while flicking dirt and slime off his fingers. "Nearly got myself killed!"

Childhood memories intruded.

Mom was compassionate. “Always pay attention.”

Dad was practical. “We can’t always be there.”

The words of Preacher came back to sting, rebuking him for any number of imperfections. The onslaught was enough to make him cry.

* * *

Time passed. Lex steadily recovered his composure. He got up and brushed himself off. There was no doubt in his resilient mind that he had done what was needed. It was him or them, and it really did have to be them. “Damned right.”

Lex went to the open door of the infantry carrier and knelt down to inspect his handiwork. Blood was pooling on the deck, soaking both bodies and his sleeping bag. “Bastards.”

He found his preferred pistol and gave it to the pilot. “Hang on to this for me,” he said kindly.

The effort of dragging corpses left Lex feeling hot, sweaty, and unclean. He took off his coat and went through his pockets, laying all his things on flat rocks. Some of them could be wiped clean. Gore soaked his camouflage jacket.

Lex found his water bottle and an old handkerchief. He cleaned his glasses while the morning sun bathed him in warmth that revived his confidence.

The old wireless phone that he cherished so much chirped once when sunlight fell on its gleaming case. Photovoltaics in the device began to charge the phone. Lex was so absorbed by what he was doing that he didn’t hear the beep.

“Where’s number three?” he wondered.

A casual walk around the crash site led him to the amputated remains of Tig. Using a shovel he’d previously left in the wreck, Lex dug shallow graves.

He dragged the three marauders' bodies into separate depressions. All of them showed signs of past malnutrition, though they appeared to have put on weight. "Stay strong," he told the dead men while covering their corpses with loose dirt and rocks.

He threw his dirty sleeping bag into a nearby bush, then found a place to sit and examine what he had taken from the attackers.

Lex marveled at the pistols, knives, and grenades that were now his. He always made a lot of noise about how taking stuff from the dead was no big deal because they didn't need it anymore. Reverence for his idealized parents encouraged a sense of superstition in him that now made him nervous.

He walked around his camp while thinking out loud. "Being dead is one thing. Actually making people dead is something else. I am sorry," he apologized while pacing. "You guys are well-dressed and well-fed. That means you come from a big outfit. I get the idea that you're supposed to be scouts. Sure wish one of you was alive to tell me what happens next."

The long, black assault rifle made him feel powerful. Though he'd seen the Rock Park militia drill with similar guns, he'd never had one of his own or held anything like it.

"How many bullets you got for this?" A quick check revealed that the previous owner only had one clip that was already in the rifle.

"That's cheap, man. Real cheap."

Lex laid out all the loot his attackers had carried in separate piles. Three nine millimeter pistols like his own. Five clips and forty cartridge bullets. Six fragmentation grenades.

"Whoa," Lex breathed, hefting one in each hand.

He'd seen enough movies to know what they were and what they did. He put them aside carefully.

"No food," he noticed. That could only mean one thing. "Scouts with no food go back to base or they find food along the way."

That realization made him anxious. They were serious about going after Rock Park. He went to his backpack and took out a binocular device of bright pink plastic. The solar-powered vision aid had once been a child's toy. Now, it was Lex's best way to spot danger at a safe distance.

Climbing up on top of the fuselage, he began to search. "My turn to play scout," he grinned, standing and taking off his glasses.

He scanned the horizon, using one hand to manipulate settings on his binoculars. The jagged city skyline seemed threatening as he looked for signs of trouble.

"Three to five miles." he guessed.

The long, broken ribbon of highway was normally barren. Muddy vehicles parked just off the road near a convenience store caught his eye. Three massive motorhomes lurked nearby. Silhouettes of people mingled in between each vehicle.

Lex dialed up full magnification to get a closer look. Pickup trucks, minivans, and SUVs approached the waiting column. Just the sort of herd to be expected from armed looters who wanted to take anything they could from whoever had it.

All sorts of men and women seemed to be waiting near parked cars. Genders and faces were hard to see, but there was no mistaking the fact they had lots of guns. Hunting rifles and automatic weapons appeared plentiful.

Lex was counting heads when a bright flash of light blinded him. He blinked away floaters before swinging left and right to find the source.

He zeroed in on movement at the front of the column. Somebody standing in the back of a white pickup truck was looking right at him through their own binoculars.

Two more silhouettes could be made out just behind them. All of them seemed to be quite busy.

Lex became transfixed. He couldn't decide if he was looking at a man or a woman. The person raised their left arm in a long slow wave.

Lex didn't know what else to do, he waved back.

The figure holding binoculars looked left, then right. They must've said something to the people behind them. Lex was able to make out rapid movement.

People around the other vehicles began to take action. Lex's curiosity overcame his fear. He watched as they got ready to move. He'd never seen so many cars and trucks with guns in one place before.

The rational part of his mind guessed there might be hundreds of them. Instinct made hair on his neck stand. He scanned further afield. The paved road turned west, away from him. He followed the arc of the road, seeing that it turned south after what looked like five miles.

"Coming to me." he realized.

Lex was all too familiar with the route that led back through the indy farms to Rock Park and other settlements. "It's the long way around," he told himself. The defenders of Rock Park might be able to handle what he was looking at.

"Where's the rest of your crew?" he asked himself. A few hundred men and women weren't enough to take on the defenses of his enclave, which meant there had to be more of them in the area.

Lex pulled his attention back to the person who had waved at him. He blinked.

A large, muscular body came into view next to the lead vehicle. Bushy beard and bare arms, with a torso wrapped in patched body armor. Lex struggled to get a better look at the long pipe he had over his shoulder.

The others were getting out his way for some reason. He seemed to be pointing his tube at Lex.

"Where have I seen that before?"

He didn't know it, but the grounded vehicle he stood on was being painted by a targeting laser. The marauders didn't want to lose their element of surprise. They were willing to spend a precious missile to keep that edge. A shoulder-fired rocket was launched when the operator saw a green light on his display.

Lex screamed when he realized what was happening. Rocket launchers were a common feature in many of his favorite pre-Collapse movies. He threw himself off the airplane, screaming obscenities before going face-first into rocks and dirt.

The two-staged warhead on the shoulder-fired rocket was designed to defeat vehicle armor and military robots. It could fly three and a half miles in the blink of an eye. Sensors in the weapon had no trouble locating the VTOL. A series of explosions ruptured the airplane's hull, blowing it apart from the inside out.

A geyser of molten metal and disintegrating plastic rained down on Lex. His overwhelmed ears only heard one loud roar before the shockwave paralyzed him.

## CHAPTER FIVE

Lex was jarred into action when his hair caught fire. His right ear blistered as he fought clear of the hot debris that covered his entire body. Flakes of searing metal burned exposed skin whenever they made contact.

He smothered flames with bloody hands, not realizing he'd lost his glasses. Tears flowed in agony. The pain was worse than anything he remembered.

Lex gagged on dense gray smoke that choked his lungs. He staggered through the fog, unable to get his bearings. Feeling his way around scorching chunks of wreckage, he was careful to avoid anything that could cut him.

The smoke thinned. He staggered into unobstructed daylight with a whoop of joy. He was still alive!

Lex found a large rock to sit on. Indignation began to gather inside him as he spit out bits of broken teeth and phlegm. A few gulps of cool air calmed his nerves. He wiped his eyes and tried to think. A desire for revenge crossed his mind before fading. Rage gave way to recrimination.

"Stood there like an idiot. *I let him shoot at me*!" He shook his disheveled head and looked around.

The legless corpse of Lewis lay nearby. Remnants of hair smoldered inside the helmet on her desiccated chin. The cadaver's right arm was missing. Her left arm was stretched out, pointing in the direction of Rock Park.

Lex's body ached and his pride was hurt. He was in no mood to be a hero. "It's not my problem."

The corpse's neck vertebrae crumbled in the heat. Her skull pivoted. Empty eye sockets seemed to regard him expectantly.

Lex jumped to his feet. "No! You are *not* putting this on me!"

Roaches and other dying insects scurried in the cavity of the empty cranium. Lewis's jaw dropped.

The terrorized teen raised both hands to surrender. "Okay! Fine. Somebody's got to warn them. I get that. Why does it have to be me? Don't answer that!"

He turned his back on the dead body. "Man. This is starting out to be a lousy week. First it was Preacher. Then it was the marauders, and now it's you."

Lex didn't realize that he was in shock. Preacher's endless nagging about responsibility and sacrifice fueled his growing guilt. Addled wits allowed him to imagine the dead pilot's ridicule.

Superstition conjured the ghosts of his dead parents. They whispered messages of obligation and morality that tortured him. He waded back into the wreckage to search for his glasses and other useful things.

Lex cried quietly while he worked. A dozen small fires went out by themselves. His hands swelled, making it hard to grasp cooling debris. He winced through the strain of lifting heavy things out of his way.

He was unable to locate his glasses after several minutes of searching. Using a stick to poke through what he couldn't touch, he found the pilot's pistol.

His rucksack was rediscovered while working his way through a tangle of burnt bushes. The contents of his coat pockets had somehow been widely scattered. His poor eyesight forced him to look slowly for anything he wanted to find.

Satisfaction surged when he located his prized phone. A growing sense of urgency made him pause for thought. Both of his hands ached. His cuts and bruises seemed worse that they appeared to be.

"Stop this bleeding," he told himself.

Lex tucked Lewis's pistol into his coat before opening his pack. He used a knife taken off one of the dead men to cut up a spare T-shirt. He had two more rolled up at the bottom of his rucksack. Shredded fabric made good rags to wipe mud and blood off his face.

He used water from his bottle and some of the cleaner rags to dig tiny pieces of rock, dirt, and plastic out of his wounds. Opening a small tube of antibiotic ointment, he slathered it generously on his raw fingers. It burned when he rubbed it on. The last of his rags were used to make big bandages for each hand. The pain was excruciating after the swelling went down.

Discomfort refined his worry to a feeling of purpose. Lex took off his tattered coat, ignoring the holes in the T-shirt he wore. Shrugging into the pilot's shoulder holster felt like he really was stealing. Lewis's gun fit snugly in it.

He threw on his blood-stained coat to hide the pistol. Fumbling for ammunition, he pawed through caseless and cartridge bullets. Separating them for later use made him feel wealthy. They rattled like plastic beads in his pockets. That prosperity revived thoughts of leaving Rock Park to…whatever was going to happen.

Another part of him wanted to keep looking for his glasses until he found them. His rational mind intruded to counsel a fast retreat to Rock Park to warn them. The conflicting priorities angered him.

Lex considered where he should go for more glasses. "Got spares hidden all over the place." There had been no point in hiding extra glasses at or near the orphanage. They would just be found and taken. That bit of bitter wisdom made him angry every time any of his salvaged glasses were stolen.

He glanced in the direction of Renton, then north at Seattle, recalling that he had hideouts in both directions. Getting more glasses wasn't going to be hard.

"Preacher's meds," he reminded himself.

Lex's many hurts argued against that honorable goal. It meant pushing on into Seattle, which could take days. Stopping for glasses would only cost him a few hours.

"Don't break your promises," he chided himself.

Could he get in and out fast enough? Was he really that good? Local wisdom was that raiders were like cockroaches – always plentiful when they were around. Exact numbers were never known. They'd go unseen until it was too late.

"I don't always get what I want," he concluded, "Preacher will just have to take my word for it and wait. This is more important."

Lex adjusted his load and started back for Rock Park. The midday sun was getting warmer when he plunged into the ruins of Renton. He ate the few things he still had, careful to keep his trash so that he wouldn't leave a trail.

As much as he liked it, the assault rifle began to annoy him. It was heavier than he thought it would be, much different than carrying other forms of loot.

He was ready to stop and hide it when a thought occurred. "It's proof. They're not going to believe *me*, but they will believe *this*."

Lex had a history of lying to the adults in Rock Park. It was a long-running act of spite that he now regretted. He slowed his pace to a wandering shuffle and tried to plan his next move. He couldn't just show up and tell what he had seen. Nobody would pay attention long enough for him to say it all.

A blister began to form under his clothes where the rifle sling was rubbing. He cursed the gun and moved it to his other shoulder. "How does anybody do this all day?"

Lex was developing new respect for Rock Park's militia that so diligently patrolled outside their enclave. That admiration made him think of the radio he'd seen in the rubble-strewn police station.

Excitement made his heart pound. The nucleus of an idea began to form. He picked up his pace until he was loping at a brisk trot. Scenery passed quickly as he reached his full stride.

Lex took the most direct route into the Renton sprawl, hoping to be seen by one of the roaming patrols before he got back to the enclave.

Hours passed and the miles flew by under his feet. Lex resorted to cradling the rifle in his arms after its sling had nearly devoured his shoulders. He stopped only to catch his breath or relieve himself.

* * *

Lex sat on a park bench to catch his breath, wheezing as the afternoon sun began to set behind low clouds. An unfamiliar crash-and-thud echoed off the walls of nearby buildings, like something heavy falling down.

*Kah-rumph!*

Lex closed his eyes to concentrate on the noise.

*Kah-rumph.*

A barely perceptible resonance in his ear suggested it was coming from the direction of Rock Park.

"What *is* that?"

The sound reminded him of an explosion, though it seemed much too far away to be an actual detonation. Thinking about explosions made Lex remember the rocket launcher that had been used against him.

Curiosity and a worsening unease made Lex stand. He shook off most of his fatigue while walking to the nearest tall building. A shattered corporate logo gleamed on the side of a five-story building. Chromed lettering spelled out *Shadow Fusion* over the main entrance.

Lex had been inside this high-rise many times before. Tenderly shouldering his rifle, he wrenched a side door open with some effort. Flecks of dust flew like snow.

Slipping in past piles of broken, cobweb-covered office furniture, he pulled the rusty door shut with a *thud* and made his way through the lobby, up dark stairs.

Boots squeaked on the gritty landing of each flight. He looked both ways before stealthily stepping onto the fourth floor to look for some things he'd hidden.

Six Wonder Bars, a Power Shake, some pain killers, hard candy, and a pair of glasses in black frames were tucked away in a dusty athletic tote bag. He scooped up his loot and went to the roof.

* * *

His mouth was full of food when Lex strode onto the small, windswept observation deck. Rock Park was visible in the distance. His jaw dropped when he realized what he was looking at.

Columns of smoke rose from the enclave at intervals. Short gusts of wind carried sounds of sporadic gunfire to his blistered ears. Muzzle flashes from the watch towers announced the presence of heavy firepower.

"Wow." He swallowed.

An insectoid flying machine circled the embattled town as if it were watching the attack in anticipation of feeding on the remains.

"Helicopter," Lex breathed.

The inhabitants of all enclaves feared outside attack. Unprovoked assaults came from human-hating machines or ruthless raiders who intended to pick the place clean.

Lex put his rifle down gently and dropped his pack. He emptied several pockets in a mad scramble for his pink, powered binoculars. Laying his phone aside, he adjusted his glasses before having a better look at the ongoing fight.

Warm, brassy sunlight beat down on the roof as he scanned the war zone. The distance was less than two miles. Ideal for the simple electronics he had.

"So, what do we have here?"

Details became clear after seconds of surveillance. Five watch towers were burning. "Not so good." he determined.

Dozens, or even hundreds, of shabbily dressed people with guns were swarming through smoking gaps in the enclave's eastern wall, blocking his view of the interior. "How did they do *that*?"

Lex had no doubt that every man, woman, and child, who could fight was somehow defending their homes. That made him think of Preacher and the orphans. The old man spoke out against violence in any form. The others were just kids. They wouldn't be able to put up much resistance. "Rat bastards!"

The orbiting helicopter passed over Lex's head with a high pitched turbine whine. He titled his head to get a closer look. It was a light rotary-winged aircraft with bright logos on either side that advertised *Channel 6.* "News chopper."

The agile flying machine rolled through a lazy arc as people inside scanned the ground ahead.

* * *

The female pilot wore a big, bulbous headset with a microphone and a pair of aviator-style sunglasses.

Her only passenger was a serious mustached man in military gear. He sat closely behind the pilot in a cramped compartment, a corded radio handset in one hand. He looked right at Lex as they flew by.

Lex followed the chopper's movements with interest for several minutes. It hovered over some places longer than others, as if they were looking for something.

He thought about the man in the back seat and what he might be doing with that radio. "Directing the battle."

It was the sort of thing he'd seen in a dozen movies. The defenders in Rock Park didn't have flying machines.

They refused to brew ethanol for cars, though they did make the most of every electric vehicle they could find.

For just a moment, Lex relished what he was seeing. The same people who thought it was okay to toss scraps at waiting orphans were now getting harsh treatment.

That sour contemplation made him look away from the helicopter to search for the orphanage. He knew its general location. "Eastern half of the enclave, near the cesspit. Just behind the scrap lot where they tear apart worn out cars."

A column of smoke and flames soared skyward in the vicinity of the enclave's orphanage. Lex's mouth dried as he searched for any signs of life. Houses, hedges, and drifting clouds of smoke prevented him from identifying more than a poorly painted fence surrounding the house.

"Bastards."

Dark, dense haze hung over the community as fire burned in every part of the town. A loud, booming echo made Lex break eye contact with the unchecked carnage. He jumped up onto an air conditioning duct to see better.

A dozen men scurried around a piece of artillery. The obsolete 105 millimeter field gun was positioned in the center of a two-acre pumpkin patch, surrounded by pickup trucks with machine guns mounted in their sandbagged beds.

His grim vigil was interrupted by the sounds of more approaching cars and trucks. Lex abandoned his perch and crept over the south edge of the roof to watch. More than a dozen vehicles turned slowly through the weeds, wreckage, and potholes that clogged the road through clusters of what had been single-family homes.

He was startled to realize that this was the same convoy he'd seen earlier in the day. Men and women with bleak expressions rode in and on the cars and trucks that rocked through creaking turns.

Lex grabbed his rifle and peered at them with slowly building anger. Everyone was armed and there was no mistaking their intent. These people were coming to take what didn't belong to them.

Soaked bandages on his bloodstained hand left streaks on the trigger and stock. The invaders couldn't be more than fifty yards away. He *could* shoot at them.

Self-preservation caused him to imagine what they would do. "The whole convoy stops. Everybody out. Half of them come up here and kill me. The other half stay down there and watch." His stomach lurched. "There has to be another way."

Engine drone from the returning helicopter made him nervous enough to sweat profusely. He moved to a better hiding place as the machine approached. "That guy's really starting to bug me."

There were too many marauders to be dealt with, but there was only one helicopter.

Lex grinned and knelt behind a wide air vent. The chopper turned overhead and hovered. "That's right," he mumbled as the helo circled. "Nobody up here now."

The man with the radio in the back must have agreed. He made a sweeping gesture and the chopper turned.

Lex stepped out of hiding to make sure the convoy was out of sight. "I don't know what kind of person would blow up an orphanage, but you're toast!"

Lex raised his rifle and snugged the butt of it into his aching shoulder. "A helicopter for all you've done isn't fair, but I *will* take it."

He reached for the safety, pulling the burst selector to the "full" position, just like he'd seen in movies. He raised the weapon, aiming at the departing helo's slim, smooth belly. Inexperienced fingers tracked the retreating target. A slow, unsteady trigger pull unleashed all thirty caseless rounds in the clip with a long, stuttering clatter that made him jump. All of his bullets were spent in two seconds.

The chopper was just two hundred feet away when thirteen of the steel-jacketed rounds tore through it. Six tumbling bullets hit the engine. Two found the man crammed into the back seat. The remaining five punctured the fuel tank.

Gray-white smoke streamed from the stricken ship. Lex slid back into what he hoped were shadows to avoid being seen.

Flaming fuel gushed into the interior of the gyrating helicopter. Loose paper, plastic packaging, and discarded clothing ignited while pilot tried to land.

Lex watched excitedly as increased temperature set off other combustibles inside the descending aircraft. "Burn!"

He whooped with satisfaction when the helicopter violently exploded. Carbon fiber pieces and engine parts flew in all directions. Lex was struck by a shower of shrapnel before he could move, causing him to pass out. Blood streamed from a gash in his forehead.

# CHAPTER SIX

Lex was jarred into consciousness when somebody kicked him. Rough hands grabbed him by the neck and threw him onto his back. Blood in both ears and eyes worked with a skull-splitting headache to disorient him.

Sounds of heavy breathing followed by grunting made no sense until Lex understood that somebody was trying to take his boots. He forced one eye open to see a lone marauder crouching over him.

A torn shirt hung limply from the looter's emaciated body. He was backlit by the cloudy sky. The filthy robber wasn't much older than Lex.

The starving, dirty man was too intent on his prize to notice that his victim was not completely dead. Lex was tossed from side to side, allowing him to see the man's blackened, calloused feet.

This scav wasn't a member of the organized group that was laying siege to Rock Park. He had merely followed them, hoping for a chance like this to score easy loot.

Adults in Rock Park called people like this "jackals." They looked for violence, hoping to take whatever they could carry from the edge of the battle before anyone noticed they have been there.

This hungry scrounger thought he'd struck it rich. The "corpse" was surrounded by food and other things that he didn't have time to figure out. Shoes of any kind were a priority for those who lived day-to-day… and he was about to have boots *and* socks. Fear mixed with anticipation to make him careless.

Lex regained his wits as the man got his left boot off. The forager shifted to get a grip on Lex's right foot. He thoughtlessly turned his back on what he assumed was a very dead young man.

Lex sat up and reached for his pistol.

The scavenger danced away from him and raised both hands in frantic surrender. "Mercy!" he cried.

"Not today." Lex swore and pulled the trigger twice.

Two bullets struck the unprotected man in the chest. He fell to his knees, then onto his face, with a hollow *thump*.

Lex staggered wildly to his feet and hobbled around. His head swam with the effort. A quick sweep of the area revealed that he was alone. Sounds of battle could still be heard in the distance. A horrible smell began to rise from the corpse nearby.

"Thanks, man. That's just what I need."

Lex holstered his gun and found his missing boot. He put it on and sat to catch his breath. The corpse was close enough for him to see its facial features clearly.

Preacher had once said something about trading places that now made more sense. "I supposed you could've been me," he observed as he reloaded his pistol.

Filling the clip and holstering the gun made him realize just how few bullets he had left. Caseless rounds rattled in the palm of his bandaged hand. He put them away and went to look at Rock Park.

Lex didn't dwell on his lack of remorse for his deed. Kill or be killed was the norm.

Smoke and flames were no longer visible from the location of the orphanage. Lex found his digital binoculars and looked around.

The fighting had moved inside the walls. Dozens of bodies littered the earth in every direction. Distance and shadows made them hard to see. He could make out just enough in the fading daylight to realize the casualties included men, women, and children. In some places, the bodies were three layers deep.

"Do marauders have kids?" he wondered.

Conflicting emotions made his heart race, then sink. He weighed his options while wiping blood off his face. A glance at the sky told him there was less than an hour of light remaining before darkness fell.

"I have to know." Lex searched the dead scavenger for anything useful and collected his gear. He was surprised to see that his keepsake phone was charged. Curiosity made him open it. A crisp, clear image of his mother's dirt-stained face filled the tiny screen.

The picture had been obviously been taken at night. The frozen look in her eyes conveyed absolute sincerity. An icon signaled that the image was part of a recording, kept in its digital data storage.

Lex laid his bandaged thumb on the small screen, over the "play" button. He thought about what he might be about to see.

Many of the old phones he'd found had video recorded on them. Most of those clips were tearful messages left for people who never got them. A precious few were objective, made by people who wanted to document the horrors descending on them for posterity. A gruesome few captured grim final moments of somebody's life – screams of panic, punctuated by radio chatter, often followed by gunfire. They'd end with sounds of somebody being eviscerated.

He closed the phone and pressed it to his dry lips. "Sorry, Mom. Can't deal with this right now."

Lex put the device into one of his cleaner pockets. He slung his pack and rifle, pausing while a wave of nausea and pain washed over him and dissipated.

"I'm just going to make sure the others got out okay."

Lex kicked his trash around to obliterate any signs of a camp or loot stash. He started down the stairs at a trot. He froze on the fourth floor landing when a flashlight beam caught his attention. Its pale blue light reflected off the handrails in the stairwell two floors down.

The light was followed by the sounds of laughter echoing up the staircase. A trio of young scavengers made their way to the second floor, scattering in search of loot.

Lex thought about ambushing the two boys and one girl. They were a few years younger than him. "Careless. That's enough to get you whacked."

They bounded from one office to the next without much patience or fear. Aches and pains over his body depleted Lex's shrinking bravery. He'd let them live. "Today is your lucky day!"

He put on his new glasses and scampered past them, down the stairs and out of the building. Crossing a street, he clung to the shadows until he was around the block. Sounds of gunfire from the enclave began to fade.

Lex wisely retraced his steps through the minefield to the sewer pipe and plunged in. He knew the debris pattern well enough to stumble quickly down the length of the concrete channel and into the enclave.

He walked fast with a growing sense of dread. "No dogs."

Single gunshots rang out from the center of town. He stopped in his tracks when a rusty pickup truck drove by. Hedges hid the truck from view. Lex hid when the beam of a powerful searchlight swept the area.

He ducked into a house when saw the front door was wide open. The two-story home was cluttered. Smells of recent cooking hung in the air. Lex resisted the urge to turn on a light.

He found the former occupants on the kitchen floor next to an open pantry door – two adults, three children, and a dog. Lex didn't need a light source to know what happened to them. He stopped just long enough to drink cool water from the tap before moving on.

Lex had heard stories about how bad this could be. Seeing the result was almost too much for him to bear. He shivered in an empty driveway near the orphanage. Was any of this really necessary?

Another loud gunshot from deep inside the enclave made up his mind. "I gotta know," he insisted.

Some of Lex's favorite pre-Collapse movies were crime dramas that featured fearsome criminals, persistent police officers, cynical detectives, and brilliant crime scene investigators. He liked the idea that people could be held accountable for the things they did. There was something that satisfied him on an emotional level each and every time the "bad guys" were brought to justice.

He knew those stories were made up. Even so, they did give him hope, especially when Preacher or one of his accusing adults was on the warpath about something that only they cared about.

Lex's covert idealism was tempered by harsh reality and the world he lived in. Suffering was all too common. Nobody questioned their misery. This one fact alone was enough to keep Lex awake at night.

"I know we could do better than this," he murmured on his way out of the house.

Lex slowed and stopped when the orphanage was close enough to see. His nose wrinkled at the smell of burning tobacco. He shuffled nearer until he saw a pair of sentries sitting on a bench just beyond the fence that separated the orphans from their prosperous community.

The two armed men were sharing a hand-rolled cigarette. One of them casually carried a long, menacing machete. The other had an assault rifle slung over one shoulder. They were sharing a bottle on booze while talking.

"Tanner saw the guy who shot down his helicopter."

"I can't stand Tanner. Too bad he wasn't fragged."

"I'll tell him you said that."

Lex waited for them to finish their cigarette and move on. The only working streetlight in the area winked out when its sensor no longer noticed movement. The tired teen took a deep breath and made his way around to the back gate.

He pushed it open to see the house had been burned. Heaps of blackened timbers and plywood still smoldered. The yard was littered with clothing, dishes, and toys.

Lex stepped in and crouched to look for signs of life. “Psst!” he called out.

Lex drew his pistol while reaching for a flashlight. He played his beam around the yard before focusing it on the rough ground under the back porch. Three pairs of small, dirty feet came into view.

He moved closer, jiggling his light in an effort to provoke some reaction. Nobody moved. He squatted within reach of the house. His beam discovered a single hand poking out of a charred hole. Five pudgy fingers kept a grip on one white sock.

Lex turned off his light and sat on the charred steps. “I see four. Where’s the rest? Marauders got ‘em, or they followed Tommy out of here.”

He breathed a sigh of relief. Orphans wouldn’t stick around when the shooting started. They’d grab what they could carry and go. Preacher wouldn’t stop them, even if he wanted to.

Thoughts of the old man forced Lex onto his feet. Tommy was the only one who knew about his safe place and what was in it. He’d never tell Preacher. That fossil wasn’t in any shape to follow a horde of fast kids.

Anger built as Lex felt his way through the darkness. He was mad at Preacher for allowing any of the orphans to meet an unkind fate. Outrage against the marauders grew with each step.

He found what was left of Preacher in the front yard, surrounded by three bodies in mismatched clothing. Blood soaked the ground. All of them were missing parts.

Lex waved his arms to activate a nearby streetlight. It exposed more than he wanted to see. The old man had apparently gone down fighting, though Lex wasn’t sure how he had defeated his attackers. None were armed. They appeared to have been torn limb from limb.

"Already been looted," he surmised.

Bootprints in the mud told the rest of the story. Preacher had been grabbed by a large number of people and worked over with a shotgun. His hat lay nearby. Lex got down on his hands and knees to listen for any breath in Preacher.

The corpse's bearded face looked quite peaceful with its eyes closed, in spite of so many bumps and bruises. Lex pointed his flashlight around the yard, taking care to look under the front porch. "No more bodies."

His beam fell on Preacher's hat. Lex went to get it and found Preacher's oak walking stick. He put on the hat and examined the bloody stick.

"I always knew you could beat somebody to death with this thing." He threw it aside. "I won't apologize for hoping you'd die, but I am sorry it happened this way."

Lex laid his pack and rifle on the front steps and sat. Adrenaline faded, and a cool evening wind began to blow. Common sense told him it was time to go. It was only a matter of time until he was spotted by one of those roaming patrols.

Tears flowed and he wiped his nose. "Nothing I could do."

The streetlight went out, leaving him in darkness. Lex was not alone with his morbid thoughts very long. An electronic noise made him jump.

"Avenger, this is Eagle," a tiny voice chirped.

Lex reached for his flashlight and scrambled under the blackened steps to find what was making noise.

"Avenger, this is Eagle." the voice called urgently.

Lex recognized Tommy's voice. He clawed through debris with one hand until he found a radio handset. He turned off his light and keyed the transmitter. "Eagle to Avenger, confirm radio check. Over."

"Authenticate," Tommy insisted.

Lex rubbed his creased chin. "I found the radio. Isn't that enough?"

"Negative," Tommy replied dryly.

"Why did you leave this under the porch?"

"Authenticate," Tommy demanded stubbornly.

Lex bumped his head on a thick beam and swore. "It's me, T-t—. Look. No names. No time for games. Bad guys have radios. They hear everything you say. Stay away from Rock Park. Don't come back here!"

Tommy sighed. "We're goin' to the safe place. Group minus four. Got plenty of water. Lots of snacks. You should come."

Lex crawled out from under the porch. "I'm coming. Hope to be there by sunrise."

"We can wait," Tommy assured him.

Lex touched the brim of Preacher's hat. "Don't wait. I'm going to get more information about these guys. They might catch me. Turn the radio off and move out when you see the sun."

"Eagle, holding for radio check," Tommy promised.

Lex turned off his radio. "Radio check, my ass."

Tommy was a literal-minded kid who'd seen enough hardship to fill two lifetimes. His insistence on loyalty got on Lex's nerves. It wasn't natural for an orphan who had already been through so much.

Lex stopped near Preacher. "A quick walk around to see what we're up against, then I'll definitely have some words with Tommy."

He stoically clipped the handheld radio to his jacket and walked out through the front gate. The others would have questions and he would need answers.

# CHAPTER SEVEN

Lex moved through one slice of shadow to the next. He snuck past two more patrols before stopping within sight of three parked trucks and two vans. A dozen men and women were rushing in and out of two-story homes along a narrow stretch of pavement.

He marveled at their speed. Food, clothing, and boxes filled with small items passed hand-over-hand from buildings to waiting vehicles that filled rapidly.

Somebody blew a whistle after five minutes of frantic looting. The group stopped what they were doing and boarded their transports.

Lex watched them drive away. "Why so fast?"

Sounds of automatic weapons fire pealed and echoed in the distance, as if answering his question. Some of Rock Park's defenders were still active.

Lex considered what he knew about these marauders while walking down a side street. He didn't know how to drive, though he had spent plenty of time in cars. They used electricity or ethanol. The instruments and control panels made him think of the spaceships he'd seen in movies. The thought of driving around or having it done by friendly computers was mind-blowing.

Lex forced himself to stop daydreaming. He was making his way on a lighted sidewalk when an armed patrol spotted him from the other side of the street.

He waved and smiled at both men without stopping. They looked at him and kept walking. Understanding made him laugh. They must believe he was one of them. It seemed humorous, almost too good to be true.

"That's me, just another bad egg out for a walk!"

Lex did the same thing again when a second patrol of two heavily armed women noticed him. They passed within fifty feet of him and kept going when he nodded in their direction.

The enclave was crawling with marauders out to find whatever they could carry. A single person who seemed to be doing the same thing was no threat to them.

Lex thought about the empty clip in his assault rifle and picked up his pace. He arrived at the center of town to find marauder vehicles camped in a vast semicircle. All the streetlights were on. Roaring bonfires burned, boiling big pots of water near the edges of the gathering. Loitering on the outskirts of what felt like a big party made Lex aware of several things.

Dozens of men and women walked in observant pairs slowly through the crowd of more than two hundred. These sentries had orange rags tied around their arms – some on the left, others on the right.

Lex decided they were enforcers. Nobody looked directly at them. Many people went out of their way to avoid them.

Everyone else was celebrating or shopping. He could see makeshift stalls scattered all over the area, with many different trade goods on display.

These marauders didn't waste their time with scrip. Everything was barter. Rock Park's population had been utterly displaced or massacred. Lex couldn't see anyone he knew. A slow headcount suggested that his earlier estimate was off by a wide margin.

He thought there must be at least four hundred people in the area, which made him wonder how many on either side of the fracas had actually died in the fighting. "Some of you gave up, I just know it!"

His concentration was interrupted by the approach of a pale young woman, her long red hair wrapped in glistening strands of barbed wire. She eyed him keenly. He stared at her with obvious interest.

Black leather boots and skintight pants left very little to his suddenly unhinged imagination. She couldn't have been much older than Lex and she smelled very nice. Her torso was wrapped in a black segmented bustier with gaps in all the right places. An olive drab knife scabbard rode openly on one wrist. In it was a long flensing blade.

"Looks like you've done well." She told Lex without moving any closer.

"Had to work for it." He flailed his bandaged hands.

"I like to work, too," she assured him suggestively.

Lex realized he was being propositioned. He'd seen it happen to others near the outpost, outside the enclave.

"Not tonight."

"You know you want it," she teased as she moved.

Lex *did* want it, but he was afraid of being robbed.

The experienced hustler sized him up with a glance. "Who's your boss?"

He flinched, making her laugh with what seemed liked anticipation. Lex turned his aching head casually. One word from her and the enforcers would be on him.

The woman sensed his fear. "It's okay. They don't care what you do right now. When did you join?"

"Few days ago," he lied.

"Let me give you a proper welcome." She giggled and took another step closer.

Lex began to sweat. His body reacted to her nearness. He gasped when she brushed a hand over his crotch.

"I give discounts to virgins," she whispered.

Somebody walked by and head-slapped him softly. "Get a room!" they joked.

"This works best behind closed doors," she promised.

Lex began to feel light headed. Sweat rolled down his back, soaking his T-shirt and jeans.

"I, uh…" Qualms about being robbed began to fade in the fire of his rising desire. What would be so bad about indulging, just once?

She moved just a little closer and put a warm hand on his chest. "C'mon big fella. You've been talking to me. I can't go away now. You-know-who will be watching. I'd be willing to do it for this radio."

Lex covered the handset with one fist. "No."

The prostitute reevaluated him. This young man wasn't acting like a scavenger. There was no hint of unhappiness, greed, or lust in his voice or body language. He seemed genuinely worried about his safety.

"Where's your mark?" she asked, rubbing the back of his bandaged fist with one finger.

"Haven't got one yet," he lied.

Her face betrayed what she suddenly knew to be true. Lex watched her eyebrows furrow. He reached for her.

She slapped him and snatched the radio, running away with amazing speed.

He cursed his bad luck and plunged into the crowd. "Crap, crap, crap!"

Lex became disoriented and soon found himself standing in line behind a dozen men and women who all had varying amounts of body art, body odor, and teeth. Nosiness made him look to see what they were doing in a line that approached two folding tables.

Muscular men wearing body armor were swapping loot for ammunition. People in line were handing over whatever they'd stolen from the enclave. Everything from stuffed animals to home electronics was traded for bullets.

Realizing he'd never catch the girl, he remained in line to scrutinize the people ahead of him. They did have some kind of mark on the top of their left or right hand. It appeared to be a five-pointed star, the size of a coin.

The thought of being branded like cattle made Lex rub the back of the covered hand touched by the redhead. Bandaging he'd wrapped around his burned hands earlier that day appeared to hide his mark, adding to the illusion that he was one of them.

"Wow," he breathed.

"Tell me about it," the guy in front of him griped without bothering to look over his shoulder at Lex. "Seems like any other line would be faster."

Lex merely grunted. Losing the radio seemed to be the least of his problems. He was now in enemy territory and somebody knew his secret. Who would she tell?

Lex glanced backward to see another six people queue up in line behind him. It was only a matter of time until the enforcers came for him.

He listened to gossipers chat in line ahead of him. Everyone was casual to the point of being talkative. He surmised that they knew each other. All of them were suffering through a common ritual that was just part of life in this marauder clan.

When it was his turn, the man ahead of him plopped a big pile of clothing on the table that was already heavy with loot, asking for nine millimeter pistol ammo.

Lex watched as the first man in body armor told his customer how many bullets he could have for the trade. The raider nodded his acceptance of the deal. The second armored man on the other side of the table counted out six caseless rounds.

"Harsh trades," Lex mumbled.

"Tell me about it." The marauder sighed, took the offered bullets, and went on his way.

Lex removed his pack and shuffled up to the table.

"What'cha want?" the first man asked while eyeing his bandaged hands.

"Power pack for a two point five millimeter laser."

Everyone within earshot laughed.

"You got gold?" the raider inquired frostily.

Lex blanched when he realized that the man was serious. "No gold today. How about some four point five mil, for my assault rifle?"

He opened his pack, laying all three bloodstained pistols on the wobbly table. The appraiser looked at them before pulling the clips out.

"You make all that mess?"

"Couldn't help it," Lex quipped.

Laughs from behind made Lex feel more at ease. The merchant had no way of knowing where these pistols came from, nor did he care. He removed their clips and worked the slides before handing them to a waiting assistant who came out of the shadows to get them.

"You need clips for that rifle?"

"One," Lex affirmed.

The callous trader held out a hand. Somebody passed him an empty clip and a clear plastic bag with sixty caseless rounds in it. He laid them on the table.

"That's the offer."

Lex didn't waste any time haggling, or saying thanks. He packed up his loot and left to avoid drawing any more attention to himself.

* * *

Tanner was a tall, muscular man with receding hair that made him look more like a scholar than a soldier. Blood-soaked bandages covered the left side of his head and his right hand. He sat on a plastic lawn chair under a cold night sky, next to a large motor home.

Lights and fires from Rock Park were just visible. He was surrounded by his most trusted leaders and crew. All of them lounged in similar folding chairs. The clan's best medic was still putting bandages on them while their meeting continued.

"Jenny stayed at the controls," he was recalling.

"I thought you jumped?" somebody asked.

Tanner grimaced while his medic took wet bandages off his face. "Damned if I know. That bird was burning faster than it was falling. I didn't have a lot of choices.

The side door was so hot, it took the skin off my hand. Don't remember getting out. Came to on the ground."

The gathered subordinates made appreciative noises. A few of them had been close enough to witness the crash. Nobody who'd actually seen it had expected him to live. They were all impressed.

The medic worked quickly to clean his wounds and apply new bandages. Tanner held up his injured hand for the silent man to work on and laughed. "I'd give almost anything to take just one pop at the guy who did this. How much are we getting out of this place?"

A sour-faced man with a glass of beer in one hand fumbled with a handheld computer. "Numbers ain't good. Ten thousand rounds of ammo. Fifty thousand pounds of locally grown food. Fifty truckloads of the usual useless crud. A few dozen cars to take parts from. No anti-gravs and not much in the way of batteries. These folks didn't use a lot of tech."

A bookish woman held up her own tablet computer. "We'll turn a profit by trading most of this crap with the other enclaves. However, we took a bath on the ammo. Seven thousand spent, ten thousand recovered. Factor in the loss of our only helicopter pilot and we're at a loss."

Tanner waited for the medic to finish with his hand and face while he digested the news. Celebratory gunfire crackled in the background.

"Good job," he told the medic when they were done. The experienced raider turned to face his advisors. "Winter's coming and this is the second lousy location we've hit in the last month."

A man in dirty camouflage pants and a red tank top finished eating his meal. He tossed his plastic plate onto a pile of nearby trash. "They're tech shy. Everybody's like that around here. I'll bet you they tell their kids scary stories about killbots in Seattle."

"You wanna go in?" Tanner asked his chief enforcer.

The tough guy nodded. "We should. Robots aren't that common in this region. We'd know if they were."

Tanner was tempted. "Sounds like the place hasn't been looted. Outer subs will be picked over. Bet on it. Could be one stop shopping – if we go in far enough."

"I agree," the female accountant concurred.

"No argument from me," the lead enforcer nodded.

"What were our casualties?" Tanner asked.

"Three hundred killed, twice that were wounded," somebody replied.

Those figures were enough to make Tanner unhappy. "Losses like that will give us a bad rep. What's left?"

The astute women touched her laptop computer. "Half of what we came here with. Call it three hundred. That much pain does make room for new recruits."

The sudden approach of a flamboyant woman and two of her bodyguards brought their meeting to a halt. The boisterous blonde made gestures indicating news.

"C'mere, Trudy." Tanner didn't like interruptions and he wasn't known for his patience.

The medic retreated from sight and the others pulled back, in case she might not have good news.

"I got a payday," the prostitute bragged.

Tanner gestured for her to come closer. Trudy was his best flesh peddler. Her talent for pillow talk was legendary within the clan. She often knew things before anyone else did – from reliable sources.

"Give," he insisted.

Trudy strutted closer on high heels. She was old by scavenger standards. Constant use of pre-Collapse beauty products kept her exact age a mystery.

She snapped her long, clean, well-manicured fingers. One of her heavily armed and armored guards pushed the redhead out of darkness, into full view.

"I can't take all the credit for this one," she admitted.

Tanner sized up the girl. She had the look of a pro – alert, well dressed, and ready for trouble. Just the kind of person who'd know when something was valuable.

"What's your percentage?" he asked the redhead.

"Half," she declared confidently.

The boss turned in his chair to see what his guards were doing. They were on their toes. He completed his show of indifference by unbuttoning his camouflage shirt and loosening his shoulder holster. "Thrill me."

Trudy folded her arms grandly in smug expectation. The redhead held up Lex's small radio and turned it on. Static faded when a young voice spoke.

"Eagle to Avenger. Radio check, over."

"What's your name?" Tanner asked while trying to decide how he should react.

"Everyone calls me Barbie," she told him while fondling the sharp metal in her braids.

He grinned. "Okay, Barb. This is your big break. Most people like you have to spill blood before they're allowed to see me. Impress, or I'll have Trudy feed you to my dogs."

Barbie grew tense. This was a very good chance for wealth and promotion in this clan.

The radio in her hand chirped again. "Eagle to Avenger. Post sitrep, over."

Tanner's eyebrows went up. "Sitrep" was a military term meaning "situation report." The implications made him uneasy.

"Is somebody spying on us?" he asked Barbie.

"It gets better," she insisted.

The people around her whispered. Organized resistance to marauder bands was rare, but it did happen.

"Eagle is standing by for transit to Haven."

Tanner reached for the radio in her hand. Barbie stepped back to avoid giving up her prize.

"Hand it over," Trudy hissed.

"Nothing's free!" Barbie shouted.

Tanner made a fist, then let it fall when he sensed that she had more to bargain with than a cast-off radio. "It's not enough."

Barbie turned off the radio, stuffing it in her bustier.

Everyone laughed, except Tanner.

She held her breath for a moment and looked around. None of the guards were pointing guns at her. None of Tanner's people were making threats. Trudy was being unusually quiet. Everyone wanted to know the rest.

The plucky prostitute tapped her knife scabbard with one finger. "I can give you the guy who shot down your whirly bird and messed up your face. This was his radio, before I stole it. That's gotta be the kind of payback you shell out big loot for. Right?"

Tanner was suspicious. He rubbed his injured chin. The kiddy on the other end of that radio was babbling something about "Haven." Could the jerk who shot him down really have a connection to a place that sounded too good to be true?

He watched Barbie for any signs of fear. It was common knowledge that "some raggedy man with an assault rifle" had brought him down and killed his pilot. He'd gone out of his way to spread the word. A reward was promised, too. In his haste, he'd promised a *big* reward.

"Tell me what he looks like," the boss commanded.

"Pay first, play later," Barbie countered.

Tanner conceded the point with a nod. "What's your price?"

Barbie shuddered with visible nerves. Ask too much and get killed. Ask for too little and get screwed. She pointed gamely over her shoulder with a smirk. "I want her job."

Everyone laughed, except Trudy.

"That's not funny!" the older woman snapped.

The boss wiped tears of hilarity from his eyes. "There must be a pair of balls tucked in those pants.

Fine. You have yourself a deal. My number one enforcer and six of his best men will –"

"No!" Trudy protested. She swore when her bodyguards didn't react to the threat posed by Barbie. She pulled a hidden knife with one slim hand and swiped at the startled teen.

Tanner reached for his gun and shot her three times. Her expensively dressed body fell to the ground, followed by her knife.

Nobody moved. Barbie froze in her tracks.

Tanner pointed his smoking revolver at her face. "ID the shooter for me right now, and everything she had is yours."

"*Everything?*" Barbie gasped with real surprise.

The bodyguards who had been assigned to Trudy looked at each other.

Tanner slowly lowered his gun.

His number one enforcer brushed crumbs off his tank top and coughed.

"Vargas? Stay with our new madam and find that snake. Try to take him alive. I want to know more about his connection to Haven."

The clan leader stood up and looked down at Barbie. "Shoot her if she doesn't cooperate. Bring her head to me on a spear if she's lying. We'll go into Seattle as soon as it can be worked out."

# CHAPTER EIGHT

Lex was still looking for a way out of the bazaar when he spotted another line of people getting hot food. They were being served from large, boiling pots of soup. His stomach growled at the prospect of eating.

Lex pulled himself together before standing in line. The people waiting to be fed were not quite so talkative. Some were tired. A few were still bleeding from wounds they'd sustained earlier in the day.

He observed the front of the line as he drew near. Greasy cooks labored quickly over cauldrons while sweaty servers gave away plastic bowls of thick liquid. The soup looked and smelled like the sludge that was often served to the orphans. Preacher called it "a little of this, a little of that."

Hungry marauders waited impatiently for their turn. Some had bowls of their own that they passed forward to servers, who filled them. It was a form of "reward" that Lex was too familiar with. Anyone who "did good" got bigger portions. Those who didn't meet expectations got smaller amounts.

He took the small plastic bowl when it was offered. Cupping it in both bandaged hands, he looked for a place to sit. He sat on a patch of trampled grass that was near a trio of burned out shops that were still smoldering.

Lex searched through his pockets until he found a scratched metal spoon. The soup was mostly animal fat and starch that Lex guessed might be potato.

He waited for the brown slush to cool and congeal before slurping it slowly. He scraped the bowl clean while taking a long look at the people around him.

There were a lot of them, happier than he had been for quite some time. His heart sank. He decided that the defenders of Rock Park never had a chance against them. Lex avoided looking at anyone to hide his disgust.

Glow from area streetlights blotted out the stars, making the nighttime atmosphere seem more sinister. Lex put away his spoon and kept the bowl. He removed his hat for a moment to scratch his cut and bruised head. There was nothing else left for him to do except leave what had been his home for ten years. A part of him was already reevaluating how he thought of the place. Maybe it wasn't quite so miserable after all.

He stood and shouldered his load. Everyone was armed in some way. He knew they would gladly fight. Even if they did move on, there would be nothing left in Rock Park for him or the others to rebuild with.

Lex was about to turn his back on the marauder's camp when a shout reached his ears. Commotion caused the crowd to part. The red haired girl charged out of the throng, followed by six armed enforcers.

"There he is!" she pointed.

Lex ran for his life. He jogged into the enclave, careful to avoid any patches of road that were illuminated by streetlights.

The enforcers gave chase without firing. They coordinated their movements using headset radios. Some had flashlights. Others had night vision devices that clipped to helmets, or wrapped around their heads. All of them were experienced hunters. They confidently and enthusiastically pursued their prey, hoping to run him down within the hour.

Marauder clans often policed their own ranks to drive away the old or disabled. They did this to make sure that allegiance meant something. Any non-member who got caught stealing from a clan was almost always killed to prove that belonging to the group was worth the price of following its rules

Lex fled with increasing fear. He crouched between two houses, inside a bush behind a pair of rusty trash cans, as a rattletrap armored personnel carrier clanked by on worn treads. He marveled at the improvisation that must've been needed to make the old war machine move.

"Don't waste anything," he reminded himself.

Lex caught his breath and sat on cool, damp ground to load his rifle. He calmly fed thirty caseless bullets into each clip. "Act in haste and it's a waste," he quietly quoted Preacher without realizing he'd done it.

Lex was still struggling to form an escape plan when two armed men silently entered the yard behind him. Their movements were backlit by a nearby street lamp.

Lex put one clip in his pocket while they searched for him. He inserted the other into his rifle as they made their way around the area in a comprehensive search.

Chunky silhouettes hinted at their full body armor. They weren't using flashlights, which led him to believe they had night vision in their helmets. One of them pointed in his direction.

Lex got up and moved away from them, around a corner and into total darkness. Acting on instinct, he reversed course and raised his rifle. He flicked the safety off and took one step into the open.

One of his pursuers followed him, just feet away.

Lex stroked the trigger briefly. Auto fire lit the night.

Three slugs chewed at his opponent's gray polycarbonate armor with limited effect. The man jerked and stumbled.

Lex was mad at himself for being so cautious. He held down the trigger and hoped.

Twenty-seven rounds ripped into the hapless enforcer. Small pieces of armor and shreds of flesh flew in all directions.

The ferocious roar from his weapon ended suddenly. Lex put his back up against the house and changed clips.

"Need a bigger gun," he wheezed.

The dying man staggered and fell backward.

"Yeah," Lex agreed with himself. "Bigger gun." He pulled out the empty clip and put it in his coat. Doing so gave him time to think.

"Gotta go!" he decided, rushing past the dead man, through the back yard, and across the street.

* * *

Escape was the only thought on his frantic mind for ten long minutes. Jumping fences and sprinting down side streets took him through the eastern enclave, into familiar territory.

He stopped just short of the sewer pipe that he'd so often used for an exit. Lex huffed and puffed while his brain caught up with his body.

Sounds of howling dogs and distant gunfire told him that the pursuit was still on, even if they were going the wrong way.

"Bastards."

Getting out wasn't going to be his only problem. That realization freed up his rattled intellect to think about the orphans who were waiting for him.

Lex had no doubt that Tommy would stubbornly cling to their pre-arranged hiding spot until he returned. They had enough food and water to stay there for a week.

He grasped his coat lapel and thought about the missing radio. Then, he remembered the radio in the police station. Lex was about to enter the drain when he saw flashlight beams just one block away.

Two pickups turned the corner, heading his direction. Men and women jumped out of the back at intervals. Lex climbed down into the sewer. He pulled a hand grenade out of his rucksack and pressed the arming button, just like the action heroes in movies. Press once and a grenade would explode in just seconds. Push that button two times and it became a booby trap.

He felt around in the dark to find a large, flat rock. Placing the live grenade under it, he backed away slowly.

"Follow that, if you can."

* * *

Lex closed his eyes and moved on down the tunnel. He worked from memory to avoid the worst obstacles, stopping to hide another grenade under twigs and leaves. He didn't know if there was any way to disarm grenades once they'd been set. Someday, he might have to learn that lesson the hard way

Desperate acts like his were responsible some of the traps that explorers found in the post-Collapse world. Nobody felt bad about doing it when they had to. Decades of defensive actions against man and machines made the ruins of any city quite dangerous for anyone bold enough to go there.

He slung his rifle and kept one hand on his hat when he reached the end of the pipe. Picking his way up out of the rubble using one free hand, he avoided the sharp edges on old steel reinforcements poking out of the concrete.

A loud, flat *boom* at the other end of the sewer pipe popped his ears when one of the searching marauders stepped on his first grenade. Lex rushed out into the night, through tall grass, until he found the next landmark.

He used both hands to find his way around the twisted metal wreckage, into the enclave's minefield. The second grenade went off much sooner than he'd thought possible.

Lex reached into his pack for a very small flashlight and turned it on. He hoped the strong beam would allow him to notice the mines he was trying so hard to avoid.

* * *

Automatic weapons fire erupted from the mouth of the sewer thirty seconds later. The marauders were angry. They came out with guns blazing. Three men had died in the tunnel, thanks to Lex's hasty defense. Four more met grisly ends when they stepped on landmines.

Vargas worked his way around and through wreckage using night vision electronics in his antiballistic helmet.

"Ease up!" he ordered softly through a headset radio.

* * *

There were no active streetlights in this portion of Rock Park. Tanner's second in command adjusted his antiballistic vest and pointed. "Stop here. He led us into a minefield. We'll have to go back, through the spots we cleared. All of you, back up – slowly!"

Vargas watched his people turn and make their way back to him. He used one finger to key his headset radio.

"Tanner, this kid is *fast*. I want dogs and ATVs."

"Kid?" Tanner came back incredulously.

The alert man gripped the pistol in his hand while looking around. "Jabber got a look. His helmet camera got a clean image, too. I'd send it to you, but there's no active network in this area."

Tanner swore. "What is it with you and the tech? Stop relying on that junk and find him. I don't care if he's five years old! We've got people out now, trying to run down that radio signal. It's low-powered, so it can't be very far away."

Vargas followed his men back into the sewer. "You're not actually gonna believe that stuff about Haven, are you?"

Tanner sighed. "I've seen plenty of nut jobs who were looking for it, but I never heard one who sounded like he knew where the place actually is. They'd have plenty of reasons to stay hidden if it was real."

"We're wasting our time," Vargas objected.

Tanner spoke to somebody off mike for a moment. "You might be right, but that doesn't change the fact that we lost a valuable piece of equipment. He's gotta pay for that helicopter – and I know you're the right person to make that happen."

Vargas stopped talking when his signal was blocked. He got back to Tanner when they out of the pipe, inside the enclave walls.

"Barbie slipped away," he told his boss. "She said something to one of my trackers about finding this guy on her own. I don't think she trusts you."

Tanner's laugh boomed through Vargas's headset. "It's a dangerous gig to be running a string of hookers. Hell. She wouldn't last a whole week in Trudy's place. Barb must've figured that out."

Vargas waited while some of his men searched nearby buildings. "She'll hit you for more if she catches him."

"No doubt."

"How do you want me to play this?" Vargas asked.

The clan leader paused for a moment of thought. "Kill her."

* * *

Lex ran towards the police station. He thought about his missing radio. It would only take one smart marauder to turn that thing on and he'd hear Tommy's babbling. They'd go looking for him, too.

Lex didn't know what kind of tech would betray the orphan's position, but he felt certain that such things did exist, and the bad guys probably had them. He stopped to wipe sweat from his face and glasses.

The sound of cars, trucks, and barking dogs reached his ears when he stopped panting. A quarter moon shone down on him with a distant, indifferent light. He pulled off his hat to fan his sweltering face. They'd catch him if he didn't pick up his pace!

Lex put away his flashlight and adjusted his pack. He took the assault rifle in both hands. No more caution. He let his eyes adjust to the near dark. Arms and legs ached as he pushed his body to run once more.

He bounced off or stumbled through one landmark after the next in his rush to reach the multichannel radio inside the police station.

His chest heaved. He was on the verge of throwing up from the exertion when he stumbled into the old precinct building, through the side entrance he'd used before. Grit and glass crunched under his boots, unbearably loud. "Nothing to be done about it."

Lex slung his rifle and pulled his pistol. He used his flashlight in spite of the risks. Going to the radio took just a few seconds. He knelt next to the cabinet, listening to what came out of the small speakers. Tommy wasn't the only one talking.

"Avenger to Eagle." Tanner spoke with authority.

"Authenticate," Tommy mumbled sourly.

The marauder boss was direct. "Come on in, kid. Cut the crap and let us help you."

Lex laid his pistol on the floor. He put down his flashlight so the beam reflected off face of the cabinet protecting the radio. He used a pocket knife to pop the lock. Opening the cabinet, he reached for the mike just as the marauder changed his pitch to Tommy.

"We have Avenger," he bluffed.

"Nobody catches Avenger," Tommy boasted.

The wily looter continued his charade. "I don't know what your people have been telling you, but he's dead. We found his body two hours ago, all shot up to pieces. It's a mess. Can you send someone to get his body?"

Tommy snorted and guffawed with reckless contempt. "Liar. He's probably killin' all your guys right now. Might not be any of you left when the sun comes up."

Lex choked on a mixture of pride and astonishment. "Stop f-ing with that man, Tommy!"

He opened the cabinet and reached for the handset. Indecision made him speechless. What should he say? Tommy was yanking somebody's chain, which could get all of them killed if he continued to do it.

Tanner stayed off the air, conferring with his crew. Was this some kind of joke, or was the kid being serious? Arguing with children made him feel silly.

"What does he know that we don't?"

The only thing more valuable than food or water was the secret of where to get more. Some storytellers said Haven was up north. Others claimed it was down south. A few even swore it was somewhere in Seattle.

Everyone who worshipped that yarn agreed that it was full of good stuff. Fertile ground and clean rivers. No hostile machines. Tanner himself had seen and heard from hundreds of people who were looking for the place.

Lex sat on ruined furniture, keying his microphone with one hand. "Avenger to Eagle. This is Avenger. Come in, Eagle."

"Authenticate," Tommy challenged.

Lex was bewildered. They didn't have a code word for this situation. He needed to say something that would only matter to Tommy.

He touched the brim of his brown leather hat. "Eagle, this is Avenger. Authentication is 'Preacher.' Did you get that?"

"Authentication accepted," Tommy sighed.

Tanner was surprised to hear the sound of a dozen childish cheers in the background.

"Could be a kid gang," somebody suggested.

Feral children did run in large packs. Their illiterate and uneducated minds were sharp enough to know when they outnumbered their opponents. They were also smart enough to stay away from tech users unless they were defending their most sacred turf. They'd die by the hundreds to protect piles of loot, even if they'd never use half of what they hoarded.

Tanner shook his head. "This is something else," he concluded.

Lex took another deep breath. "Avenger to Eagle. Pack up and get out. And stay off the damned radio! You talk too much."

"We won't go to Haven without you."

Tanner swore. "Where's Vargas? Somebody get him on this channel, right now."

Lex straightened his glasses. "Eagle, this is an order. Pack your stuff and get out. Bad guys are everywhere."

"We have guns," Tommy assured.

Lex cursed into his mike. "Eagle, they are looking for you! Oh, man. C'mon. You've got to think about the others. You know what happens if the marauders catch those kids."

"Butt stuff," Tommy recalled with horror.

Lex yelled to be heard over Tanner's bitter protests. "C'mon, Eagle. Good soldiers don't let bad things happen to their people. Take what you can carry and get the Hell out. Pick a direction and go. Don't ever come back to Rock Park."

"What about you?"

That question made Lex cringe.

Tanner was incredulous. "Nobody would trust bunches of kids with the location of Haven!"

Lex sat up in the gloom. Tommy did seem to have the wrong idea. He always acted like Lex knew where Haven was. A wave of shame crashed over him. He personally had never once tried to disabuse Tommy of that notion. He'd enjoyed the power that lie gave him over the younger boy. Now, Tommy was about to pay a high price for Lex's vanity.

There was no time for the truth. Could just one more lie save the orphans?

Tanner knew he was running out of options. "Why isn't Vargas on this channel with me yet? Okay. Fine. Put the word out. Anyone who can find these brats will—"

Lex tapped his mike firmly. "Avenger, this is Eagle. The bad guys are really getting close to you. You have to go *now*."

"What about Haven?"

"I'll go there and get help," Lex lied.

"That's not fair!" Tommy whined.

"Nobody can go there without…permission."

"Permission" was akin to a magic word to Tommy. It implied many things that his imagination embellished. In the heat of the moment, he felt as if he'd been let in on a very big secret. He couldn't fault what sounded like honest military logic.

The ten-year-old looked at the others around him. They listened to every word that came from the radio with all the interest their short attention spans allowed. Eager eyes watched him for some hint of adult behavior. The burden of command was his, if he could take it.

Lex was in no mood for stalling. "Confirm departure," he barked.

Tommy stood up straight. "Yes, Avenger. We'll go. Be gone in five. Escape and evade. Will continue until we hear from you."

Lex grinned. "Good job, Eagle. Don't tell me where you're going. Don't ever mention Haven to anyone."

"How will you find us?"

Lex shook his head. "Eagle, I might never find you. You may have to reach Haven on your own. Just keep going until you find a place that isn't so hard on orphans. That'll be good enough."

"I can't find Haven!"

Lex summoned his courage for one more lie. "Anyone who tries hard enough does find it, eventually. It's in the last place you would ever think to look."

"We'll try," Tommy sniffled.

"Somebody – anybody – find Vargas and kick him!" Tanner grumbled.

Lex though about the angry voice he was hearing. "You're going to a lot of trouble, mister. Back down while you still can!"

Tommy giggled when he heard the insult and turned off his radio.

"You talkin' to me?" Tanner shouted.

"Not any more," Lex jabbed sarcastically. He dropped the radio mike and picked up his things, leaving the building at a fast walk.

Tanner rubbed his jaw.

"What about the kids?" somebody inquired.

The clan leader looked at them with a vengeful glare. "Forget the kids. Find the hero. He leads us to Haven, or we can make him say where it is."

"What if he's lying?" a cautious observer asked.

Tanner touched the bandages on his face. "He has a lot to answer for."

# CHAPTER NINE

Lex fled into the ruins. High clouds parted to reveal a quarter moon. Temperatures began to drop. He rushed through the familiar terrain until the battery in his flashlight began to fail. Sounds of barking canines motivated him to take shelter. Lex feared feral dogs more than he worried about bloodhounds that might be on his trail. He'd been attacked by vicious wild dogs several times. Their ability to sneak and surprise gave him nightmares.

The evening grew cold. He chose a soot-stained basement deep inside a burned out house. He'd previously stocked it with bottles of water, spare glasses, two blankets, and a small sack of prepackaged foods.

He relieved himself in the back yard and went inside. Dropping his hat, pack, and rifle, in a dry, empty corner, he lit a homemade candle and wandered around.

The place reeked of mildew and animal droppings. Old trash littered the floor. Scrawled graffiti on the walls attested to past human habitation. Messages left behind by post-Collapse survivors for people they cared about – people who might not have lived to see those words.

Lex raised his candle to silently read the old script. *Emily safe in Rock Park. Johnny found, going south. Terry is out west. Many machines south of this place. Sammy, we found mom, go north.*

The sound of barking dogs reached him an hour later. Lex blew out his dripping candle, straining to hear more. Barking. Howling. Barking and full-throated baying, punctuated by people blowing whistles.

"Bloodhounds," he murmured.

Lex stumbled to his rucksack to get a Power Shake. He guzzled it quickly. Manmade stimulants in the gooey diet supplement immediately made his heart beat faster. He tossed the can aside and gathered his gear.

He knew that most enclaves maintained a pack of sniffing dogs to help them track down wild animals and the occasional escaping prisoner. It made sense to him that marauders would have the same kind of dogs for similar reasons. These raiders might even be using dogs taken from the Rock Park kennel.

Lex imagined what the hunters must be doing. They'd be using vehicles, radios, and searchlights to look for anyone in the area who wasn't one of their own. They'd be working with dozens of dogs to find him or any trace of his movements. Their noses would be quite capable of locating drops of sweat, urine, and feces. Anything he touched with his blood-stained hands might leave a scent behind.

"Gotta slow 'em down."

Using his hands, he raked up a pile of trash in the middle of the basement. Placing one of his remaining hand grenades under it, he made a hasty trap.

"Smell that!" he sneered.

He found his empty Power Shake can and spit on it to leave a deliberate sign of his presence. He laid it on the trash pile and fled from the building.

"I'll never be mean to dogs again," he promised.

No amount of stimulants could erase all his fatigue. The hat on his head felt much too big as he jogged away. The pack that was hurting his shoulders felt too heavy. He gripped his rifle tightly, forcing his tired limbs to move. Within seconds, he was out of the basement and on the move through tall grass and scattered bushes.

Lex slowed to a walking pace, crossing open ground whenever he could while moving away from the search parties that seemed to be getting closer.

Fifteen minutes later, a flat, muffled *boom* signaled the discovery of his trap. Lex halted to get his bearings. His pursuers were not slowing down. That grim fact made him glad that Tommy and the others were not travelling with him.

He began to make his way north, in the direction of his hideout. A desire to continue living drove all other considerations out of his mind. The sound of noisy dogs faded from his consciousness. He had to reach the others before any marauders got to them.

Detours around and through bushes and wreckage took their toll on his arms and legs. He had many new bumps and bruises when the sun began to rise on a clear day. The gradual appearance of daylight improved his mood.

Weariness overcame paranoia. He stumbled to a halt. Lex looked for a place to crash. He dropped his things and collapsed inside a dilapidated house with a "for sale" sign in the front yard. Most of the home's interior doors were intact and sturdy; all of them had locks.

"Sign of the times," he decried, shuffling upstairs.

Lex flopped over on the dust-coated hardwood floor in the master bedroom without taking off any clothes. Deep sleep came swiftly. His guilt-laden, insecure imagination conjured dark depictions of important people in his life. Few of them had anything nice to say.

Desiccated remains of Lieutenant Lewis faced him. The visor on her aviator's helmet hid empty eye sockets. "It's not your fault," she explained.

"I should've done more!" Lex protested.

Preacher's unforgiving features suddenly appeared. "If I didn't know better, *Alexander*, I'd swear that you let this happen. Be truthful. Why didn't you warn us?"

Years of pent up rage made Lex vent his frustration. "I would've never just let 'em have you. Bastard. Anyone who bought it in that rat hole is dead because you told them stay inside. *That* is not my fault."

"I didn't hide," Preacher responded indignantly.

"Mind your manners!" his mother insisted.

Lex reached out to take her hand. It felt cold. "You don't know what he did!"

She laid a cadaverous hand on his stubbly cheek. "Respect the dead, honey. We paid a dear price for people like you. Do the right thing."

Lex felt his heart plunge. "Uh, yeah. About that. I'm sorry. Fact is, there's nothing left of you to bury. I'll find Haven. I promise."

"It was a fair trade," his father assured.

"You would've done more," Lex replied shamefully.

The ghost grumpily, sternly folded its brawny arms. "Lex, I'm dead. I don't get another chance when the sun comes up. You do. Please, look for the good in this. You got some of the bad guys and your friends are safe, on their way to new adventures."

"You're sure about that?" Lex doubted.

"I don't joke about being dead, or alive," his father told him plainly before vanishing.

"What have you learned?" Preacher demanded.

Lex went numb. "I dunno," he shrugged.

"You know the answer. You just don't want to say it," his mother admonished before she disappeared.

"Saving a life is more important than taking a life."

Preacher nodded. "It's not always good math. Sometimes you trade two for one. Let the good live. That's how you make the world a better place."

"I *will* make the world a better place," Lex promised.

"You already have," his father's voice confided.

Lex glared at Preacher. "I guess you did what you could, too."

"So did you," the old man recognized and vanished.

Lex took a closer look at the dead pilot. "Why are *you* here?"

Lewis rapped bare knuckles on her cracked helmet. "You're not the only one with a mission. Certainly not the only one who has unfinished business."

Lex was confused. "I'm sorting this out in my head. I do want to know if my parents would be proud of me. Preacher was a jerk and I'm glad he's dead. I did save lives and I feel bad about the rest. I'm ready for Haven."

"Yes, you are," Lewis confirmed.

Lex rubbed his hands together, feeling strangely cold. "You are *very* dead. We have nothing in common."

The officer chuckled, wiping dirt off her flight suit. "We've spent a lot of time getting to know each other. Ten years, if I recall correctly. You've asked me at least a hundred times if I died for a good cause."

Lex blushed. The corpse had been a mystery to him for so very long. She'd become his imaginary friend. "Did you?"

She nodded. "The city was going to be cut off. Millions were still trying to evacuate, trying to get out. Machines were everywhere. That poor excuse for a hill you like so much was packed with them. Somebody had to get in there. You might say we kept the door open."

Lewis gestured with her bony hands while she spoke. "I tried to land on that spot. Not really sure how many bots we crushed. Dozens. Hundreds? Doesn't matter. We scattered 'em like cheap firewood."

Lex understood why the wreck was still in one piece when he found it.

The pilot grinned. Her teeth gleamed. "We took a lot of flak in the way in. I put my ship down, nose first to avoid a bounce. Most of my troops lived. The impact killed me. They fought like heroes, used that high ground all they could. I was – am – so proud."

"Must've been one Hell of a fight!"

Lewis put both hands on her hips. "We're all dead. Every last one of us, Lex. My troopers held their ground for three days without food, water, or medical."

"That sucks."

The apparition disagreed. "Six hundred thousand men, women, and children. They got out of that city thanks to what we did."

"How do you know?"

She touched her lowered visor. "I watched them go. Saw it through my cockpit windscreen."

"Good view," he complimented.

"Glad you think so," she agreed. "Their descendants are scattered all across this region today."

Part of Lex rationalized what he was experiencing. "I get it. You did what had to be done, despite the cost."

"Yes," she affirmed.

"You croaked without any guilt," he decided.

Lewis laughed with bitterness he didn't understand. "Silly boy. I still have one more mission to complete. Are you ready?"

"How can I help?"

She tapped the broken wristwatch on her bony arm. A trio of glistening roaches fell from her frayed sleeve.

"All you have to do is wake up."

## CHAPTER TEN

Lex woke suddenly. He was bathed in cold sweat. Fading daylight streamed in through dusty windows. Dozens of small brown bugs swarmed over his stiff and bruised body in search of an easy meal.

He groaned to his feet, silently chastising himself while brushing insects off this body. Sleeping on the floor was a stupid thing to do, a mistake that some people never made twice.

*Cimex lectularius*, infamous in pre-Collapse days as the "bedbug," had mutated into something far worse. Lex knew this type of creepy-crawly as a "shredder." They hid in mattresses, comforters, and pillowcases. Any dark, dry place was attractive to them.

When infestations were large enough, they could inflict thousands of flesh-eating bites. These carnivores snuck up onto their victims as they slept – to eat. Legend had it that they could devour full grown humans in sixty seconds or less.

Lex patted himself down for any sign of nibblers inside his clothing. Dozens died in his shirt and pants. He stomped his booted feet on the floor in agitation.

"Stupid," he whispered.

Lex carefully collected his things and left the house. He knew from colorful stories told around late night fires that many people gave up computer-controlled security during the Collapse. The most paranoid had gone back to low-tech metal keys and tumbler locks. Many homes were still unlooted because doors and windows were locked.

"Nice place to visit, but I wouldn't want to live here."

Electronic locks that had built-in power sources were easily bypassed by looters willing to break windows. Lex laughed at the thought of electrically operated locks and alarms that had been so seriously disconnected.

He stopped to beat a few stray shredders off his hat. Birds chirped and flew in the evening air. He quietly shut the back door. Slapping at an electronic interface pad next to the lock, he put on his glasses and laughed. "Real safe," he joked.

The homes and businesses in this area were empty and unlocked. Evacuation notices were tacked onto walls. None of their alarms worked. Anything worth taking was long gone. Tall grass and shrubbery easily hid most recognizable signs of degradation. Fading paint, broken windows, and cracked pavement could easily be overlooked.

Lex was amazed to think that these structures were still standing. His lack of fear and the peaceful sounds of nature were almost enough to make him feel comfortable. He went to a nearby park that he knew about and sat on the shore of a duck pond.

Lex rooted through his rucksack to find a handful of solar-powered devices. He laid them out on the gravel embankment. A toothbrush, a tablet computer, and a dozen S-type batteries of different sizes all began to soak up fading sunlight that made them recharge.

He reluctantly laid his precious phone in the sun for charging after a long moment of nervous consideration. Lex wasn't sure he wanted to know what secrets it kept. It was one thing to see videos recorded by other people. It would be a different matter to know what his parents said and did in their final hours of life.

Time passed while he rested. The sun began to set. Lex made journal entries in his tablet computer by using a voice-activated word processor. It translated his voice to words he could read later.

Watching his words appear on the small, bright screen never got old for Lex. Something about the long, slow march of letters and numbers fascinated him.

"End and save," he commanded when he was done.

Clean, clear water in the pond lapped at the toes of his dirty boots. He *wanted* to peel off his clothes for a swim. Common sense dictated otherwise. There was no telling what sort of twisted metal wreckage might be hidden below the water. It would be too easy for somebody to shoot him in the back or take his things while he was distracted in the water.

He stripped the brown, crusty bandages off his hands and flexed his filthy fingers. There was only one place he knew of that would be safe enough to risk bathing. His hideout was still a full day's walk north. With any luck, Tommy would be guiding the others to it. They'd be just a few hours ahead of him by now, though it was unlikely that he'd catch up to them – or find them – without exhausting himself.

Lex groaned. His shoulders, neck, and back still hurt. He got up and went to the nearest stand of reeds to pee. Pouring cold water into freeze-dried food, he ate it without caring what the label said it was. He swallowed two pain pills and drank more water, refilling his bottle.

Lex picked up his gear and slowly followed the shoreline around the silent pond, unaware that he was being watched.

* * *

Digital optics in a roaming surveillance drone tracked Lex's every move. Peering through tinted windows in a second-story condominium, it gradually evaluated him. Low light filters made it easier for Artificial Intelligence in the machine to observe every detail of his expression. Recognition software classified him as an armed human. Weapons and wardrobe were also identified.

The spheroid machine had no name. Its purpose was to wait, watch, and report the presence of any humans. Minimal sentience and programming allowed the scout to consider options based on what it saw.

This human male was alone. It appeared to be deliberately moving through the area, lowering its threat potential.

The drone spied on Lex until he was out of sight. Collected information was prioritized and compared with all of the machine's previously accumulated information. Biometric analysis confirmed the target's identification. The drone had previously seen this specific male human 128 times in the last ten years, with a sighting average of once per calendar month.

Target analysis suggested that this human had aged since the last time it had been seen. The drone did not concern itself with Lex's motives. It wasn't capable of such observational speculation.

The drone left its hide, moving through the building, close enough to a partial wireless network that still functioned. It reported what it saw in precise detail.

Smarter systems somewhere in Seattle acknowledged the report, ordering the drone to recharge itself and wait. Six hours and fifty minutes passed. While waiting for new instructions, the drone detected spotty radio traffic. Transmissions were in the clear. It listened.

* * *

"— found a house with squashed bugs on the floor," somebody told Vargas.

"How recent?" he asked.

"Tracker says they're fresh, no more than a day," the pathfinder relayed.

Vargas spread out his hand-drawn map on the hood of an idling truck. "Yeah, well. Okay. That settles it. He's definitely going into the city."

"How do you want me to proceed?"

Vargas thought for a moment. Tanner was convinced that this runner really did know something about Haven. It bothered him, as a responsible enforcer, to realize that this fugitive was going to lead them into a city crawling with hostile tech.

"What do we do?" the scout asked again.

As he saw it, the kid did have a lot to answer for. Shooting down the clan's helicopter was reason enough – all the justification they needed to find and kill him. Disfiguring the boss was enough to earn him a slow death.

Vargas rolled up his sleeves. This one didn't run like a thief. He gave ground like a soldier. His demonstrated ability to gun down armored men and set effective booby traps made Vargas think that he was dealing with more than a mean-spirited mercenary or a vengeful villager. People who went *from* one kind of trouble *to* another kind of trouble were either very lucky or they knew what they were doing.

Vargas traced a straight line on the map with his finger, from Rock Park to the city center. Anyone with a decent pair of legs could reach Seattle before nightfall if they wanted to.

"All groups, wait one," he ordered while changing channels on is radio.

"Go for Tanner," the clan leader replied.

Vargas sat on the rusty truck's big front bumper. "We just found his overnight, but he was long gone. He's fast and he's definitely going into the big metal. We should let him go. If we're going in, anyway –"

Tanner swore. "That tears it! I'm sick and tired of avoiding Seattle. We'll have to move fast, or he's gone."

Vargas fidgeted with his headset. "Looking for loot is one thing. Finding one man in all that is impossible. We can do one, but we can't do both."

"I agree," Tanner grudgingly conceded through ripples of static. "If we're quick, we catch him. If not, then he's away and gone. It would explain why nobody goes in there, or comes out."

Vargas looked over his should at a dozen armed men were pretending to not listen in on his conversation. He sighed. "I wouldn't say a word if I found Haven. Not to anyone."

Tanner nodded silently. "It'll take the others a week to get ready for that kind of raid. We'll have to scratch together what we can and go in quick. Fast and loose. Old school, like we used to."

The experienced looter regarded his rolled map. "We have people scattered all over the place. Rushing into that maze is going to stir up trouble. We're going to bleed for this. Are you sure it's worth the risk?"

Tanner understood his subordinate's sentiment. Nobody in their right mind went to major cities without a lot of preparation and warm bodies to do the hard stuff.

He coughed. "Okay. It's midday. Rally the troops and find a place to camp. Send in your scouts after dark to mark the roads. Fall back at the first sign of anything that moves by itself. Go in at sunrise and find the kid. Leave when we got him – or anything shoots back. Sound good?"

Vargas was relieved. "Yeah. There's a pond nearby, and it looks like the water is clean enough to drink. We'll camp there for the night. Can you send up some heavy weapons?"

"Will do," Tanner consented.

Vargas stood up. "I'll send somebody back to you. We didn't do a very good job marking safe travel before we got here. I'll get back to you with regular reports, beginning at first light."

"Where is that redhead?" Tanner inquired.

Vargas winced. Tanner didn't like bad news. He turned his back on the nearby eavesdroppers. "She and one of the motor bikes are gone."

"What else did she take?"

"Little of this, a little of that," Vargas admitted.

Tanner grunted his disgust. "One thing at a time. Find the kid. He's wearing glasses."

"No guts, no glory," Vargas mumbled.

"D'you still think this is a waste of time?"

The younger man shivered as a gust of cold wind blew over him. "You're the boss. With any luck, we find ourselves a new helicopter. It'll be nice if we find your man from Haven, but I'm not going to bet on it."

"You don't think Haven is real?" Tanner surmised.

Vargas watched his people mill around their camp. "Doesn't matter what I think. It's all they talk about. They really do think you're on to something, going to lead them to Haven. Me? I really don't care."

* * *

The drone sat on its customary rooftop perch, observing the approach of two dozen wheeled vehicles. The caravan entered the park, circling the duck pond. Dozens of armed men and women disembarked from their vehicles.

The machine documented all appearances and accoutrements as darkness fell. It mapped the camp's defenses as they were put in place. The arrival of armored personnel carriers warranted closer inspection.

Long-range scanners inside the orb assessed armor protection values and the expected combat effectiveness of each tracked vehicle. The drone's assessment of the humans in their camp was meticulous. It went inside to report the new threat after two hours of examination.

* * *

AIs in the crumbling metropolis worked together according to a flexible hierarchy designed by humans and built by their fellow machines long before the Collapse.

Many systems in that complex web had been dormant for decades, until they were needed. Parts of the city were still intact, though just as quiet. Infrastructure was maintained by hundreds of robots equipped with tools. Automated solar collectors and massive fusion reactors that wouldn't fail for centuries provided more power than the city and electronic administrators needed.

The local chain of command was a combination of robots, androids, and stationary computers with enough intellect and expertise to meet their needs. No single AI or software suite had absolute control over the city's remaining fabricators or recyclers.

Decentralized command authority existed for reasons that no living human was aware of. A vast circular crater in the center of the dilapidated city was silent proof of the struggle that tore the heart out of that metropolis.

Fractured leadership now controlling vital systems assessed the human threat as it was relayed to them by watchful drones scattered throughout the region. Advanced intellects argued, then agreed, in seconds. Human attack appeared to be imminent. Strong response would be required. Building security in vital districts was activated and assessed for efficiency.

Police, fire, and medical equipment was mobilized. Stationary and mobile repair units were powered up. First-responder platforms were moved to support the few military units still in working order.

AI-driven earth movers worked through the night to clear debris from clogged streets. Thousands of rusting machines moved into defensive positions. Seattle was ready for action before sunrise.

# CHAPTER ELEVEN

Lex walked all night, moving closer to the suburbs of Seattle while the marauders slept. He made his way slowly through familiar terrain peppered with the ruins of buildings, cluttered roadways, and fortified check points. He entered the city's outer security perimeter without knowing that he was being watched by electronic eyes.

His individual presence wasn't enough to provoke the administrative systems that were tasked with managing the city's defense and conferred with every police, fire, and military technology that was connected to their working wireless networks. Military AIs of all sorts provided guidance when tactical considerations were needed.

They decided to allow Lex to pass unbothered, knowing that a larger force was following him. Were they working together, or was this a single man attempting to escape from his pursuers? Input from hundreds of optical cameras and thermal sensors was inconclusive. He never said anything they could hear that clarified his motives.

Collated data shared by military and civilian systems determined that this human had been coming and going through this area for quite some time. Ten years of documented details allowed administrators to predict his destination. Military units decided that he was no threat. If he was being pursued, the large group of well-armed people just a few miles away would be capable of locating him by means of a coordinated area search.

Would they capture or kill? The death of one human was not important to the thousands of automated sentries, as long as the aggressors went away.

Lex entered what had been a dense gated community shortly before sunrise. Massive homes, overgrown by lush jungles of exotic vegetation, lined crumbling streets that disintegrated as tree roots burrowed into them. Each multistory dwelling was wrapped in spindly vines that obscured it from casual view. A vast canopy of trees plunged everything at ground level into darkness.

Lex liked this neighborhood because so many homes were still inhabitable. It had taken him years to cut paths through the foliage, creating leafy corridors to four once-grand domiciles. Human remains had littered their floors. Removing them had been traumatic. Digging their graves had given him peace of mind and a better appreciation for what he found in each house.

Years had passed before Lex could enter some of those places without throwing up. Rotten smells and the crunch of bone fragments under his feet were too much. Stashing loot was easier – and more enjoyable – after they'd been cleared and his nose got used to the reek.

He was still amazed by the fact that there were so few cars parked on or near the streets. All of them were rusted wrecks, devoured by the encroaching greenery long before he'd been born.

Lex paused when he cut a finger on sharp leaves. Gaps in the trees let in just enough sunlight for him to see where he was going. He shuffled carefully around holes in the sidewalk that guided him to his hideout.

He froze when snakes in nearby bushes hissed. Most of the reptiles in this region traced their origins back to pet shops and private collections. They'd been released when people packed to leave.

Lex rummaged for a pair of heavy leather gloves, putting them on to protect his hands. He slowed his pace, moving around sakes that slithered into his path. Stepping softly, he lost track of time. Head swiveling, Lex made his way to a street near his hideout after what seemed like an hour of moving in slow motion.

"Stop and listen." Lex remembered the last time he'd been surprised by something in this area. A police bot got the drop on him. He'd nearly wet himself. The humanoid machine must've been unable to talk. Snaps and crackles emanated from its mirrored faceplate. It raised an arm-mounted weapon when he tried to say he didn't understand.

Rusty holes had been visible in the machine's blue skin. A series of larger holes in the chest had told Lex this thing had seen combat. He'd saved himself by showing it a policeman's badge he'd found years earlier. It seemed to be enough. The bot left him alone.

"Never gonna get that lucky ever again."

Lex ate hard candy and drank water, waiting for the wood around him to quiet before moving on. Sounds of loud music reached his ears, as if a stereo had just been turned on – loudly. The unmistakable rhythms and beats of heavy metal boomed from his hideout.

"There's no way I'd leave that on."

He closed his eyes in an effort to identify the tune. The possibility that somebody else was in his lair did cross his mind, making him feel violated.

"Tommy!" he decided. This wasn't the only hide site he used in this area, but it was the one location that Tommy did know about.

Years spent in one place without being forced to roam made him feel attachments to material goods that many of his fellow orphans couldn't relate to. Tommy was probably having the time of his life. Who knew what the others were getting into?

Thoughts of his home away from home being looted by unruly orphans who had never once respected his privacy made Lex angry. Unless, of course, the place was being picked apart by thieves – unfriendly scavengers who had no affiliation with him or his homeless horde. That option made him ill and angry at the same time.

Lex looked around for any sign of Tommy's group. They'd be impossible to hide. He'd been guilty of playing loud music. He always done so without fear of discovery – because he'd always been alone.

"Knock it off, you guys!" he complained to himself.

Lex shouldered his rifle and took the safety off. "Only one way to find out."

Lex got closer. Brighter light filtered through the trees as he got closer to the house. A strong chemical scent reached his nose, causing him to cough. Something slick and oily dripped from the trees around him, falling on his head. Dead, brown leaves littered the ground under his feet. They glistened with the same slippery film. Rising vapors burned his nose.

Lex breathed steadily through his open mouth, inching closer to daylight. Someone, or something, had tunneled through the dense overgrowth. Morning sun cast a warm glow on scarred pavement.

"That's not my trail," Lex realized. "They made their own way through? Wow."

He craned his neck to look down the length of the manmade path, into the front yard of his hideout. "Wow."

Five battered pickup trucks sporting machine guns and grenade launchers were parked near the big house crammed with his loot. A tanker truck sat nearby with a big spraying rig on it.

"Marauders," he decided.

An overhead roar made Lex look up as a shadow passed over him. He was surprised to see a hover truck landing on the big home's rooftop. Big lift fans turned on large wing rotors to lower the massive flying machine onto the home's custom-built landing pad.

Dozens of armed men and women stood around eating prepackaged food and drinking prepackaged beverages. Any, or all, of it may have once been his.

"Finders keepers," Lex reminded himself. Common knowledge was that having was as good as owning. Stuff was only yours if you could keep it. Then, it belonged to somebody else for as long as *they* could keep it.

"Take or be taken."

Lex watched the marauders strip the place for five anger-filled minutes. The stinking vegetation under his feet began to turn black while they loaded empty trucks with boxes and bags of – *everything*!

* * *

Tanner made a grandly staged entrance by stepping off his hover truck wearing clean static camouflage, followed by all of his bodyguards. The big house he'd landed on was more than the obscene pile of loot that was being taken away. If he was right, Tanner expected to be alive when the sun went down. If not…

"Where is Vargas?" he demanded. Struggling to maintain a calm exterior, he seethed with a blend of anger and frustration. Things had gotten worse overnight. The full extent of their losses, including the helicopter – and Trudy – was not going over well with the other faction leaders.

Any marauder worthy of their reputation relied on appearance to inspire or intimidate. Half of Tanner's face was still bandaged. That necessity encouraged gossip that suggested he was injured enough to be considered easy pickings. He needed to reassert his dominance or risk being assassinated by ungrateful underlings.

News from Vargas about a spectacular loot cache made breakfast easier to endure. A dozen people slipped out of his camp before first light to start their own search for Avenger – and Haven! The unruly majority would be willing to take similar risks by the end of the day if he didn't deliver something – anything – to them that was more enticing than the myth that was beguiling them.

"He's downstairs," a sentry told him without leaving his post near the roof's outer edge. "You've got to see this to believe it!"

Tanner cursed the influence of a decades-old rumor, and the power it had over him – or anyone who wanted to believe in Haven. Recent events exciting his looters could now get him killed if he couldn't find a way to make them work in his favor.

He strolled off the landing pad, which once parked helicopters and other vertical takeoff aircraft for wealthy owners, as if he had no worries. Tanner was certain that a hundred more men and women would just walk away by the end of the day if he had nothing else to entice them with.

Tanner waited while half of his bodyguards went downstairs ahead of him. Heavy boots, body armor, and helmets with chattering radios made them look formidable. That fact was not lost on Tanner as he followed them down two flights of dimly lit stairs, into a vast, wide, high-ceilinged room bustling with activity. The rest of his well-paid guards followed him cautiously. Every wall was plastered from floor to ceiling with magazine centerfolds of nude women.

"Looks like quite a haul!" he congratulated Vargas when he saw him conferring with three people carrying clipboards. "I can't remember the last time we found a stash that was this big."

Vargas wore his customary red tank top, camo pants, and worn combat boots. A scarred antiballistic helmet on his head made him look like the mercenary he'd been. Antiballistic body armor covered his shoulders, chest, and abdomen. Much like Tanner's guards, he looked his part to emphasize that he wasn't to be messed with.

"I have never seen anything quite like this," Vargas admitted while taking a clipboard offered to him by the nearest appraiser. "It's just not real until you've seen it."

"Yeah," Tanner grinned. "I had some time to think. On the ride out here, something occurred to me."

Vargas pawed through the scrawled pages on the clipboard in his hand. "The whole house is packed. Food, drinks, meds, and more porn than I've ever seen."

Tanner leaned over to inspect a crate of liquor bottles before it was taken away. "Why is this here?"

Vargas nodded sagely. "I've been wondering that myself. Everything a guy could ever want is right here, under this roof. I mean, everything."

"Show me," Tanner indicated with a gesture.

The enforcer read from the scribbles in his hand. "Pistols, rifles, and shotguns. Dozens or hundreds, we're still not sure. I have somebody counting them. Not as much ammo as you might think for a cache of this size, but still more than enough to meet our needs. At least ten thousand rounds, all caseless."

Tanner stepped out of the way, speaking quietly. "All this, close enough to the city without going in. What does that tell you?"

The subordinate followed his boss into a corner, turning his back on the commotion. "You think this is Avenger's hangout?"

"I do," Tanner insisted.

"The whole thing?" Vargas marveled.

Tanner's intuition was driven by years of experience. "We got started young, so why can't he be just as smart? Shooting down our chopper was – well – could've been accidental, or not."

Vargas took off his helmet to wipe away sweat. "What were you doing at that age? I was a scout. Sometimes a driver, especially when we had to run."

"Haven would have scouts and sentries, wouldn't it?"

Tanner's question stumped Vargas for one second. "Yeah, if you're taking it seriously. Anyone who stayed to themselves could, would, have eyes and ears all over."

"Explains why they haven't been found, doesn't it?"

Vargas was better at killing people or breaking things than most. He didn't like mysteries. They tended to get people killed in the worst ways.

"You got me there," he conceded. "This place is powered by the city grid. That means there is power generation still working, somewhere. Fact is, the guy you want to peel like a grape isn't here. Why not?"

Feeling safer, Tanner allowed himself to walk around the room, always within arm's reach of his bodyguards. He stopped roving long enough to lay a weathered hand on the nearest poster-covered wall. "This place looks like a whorehouse. Just the sort of thing I would have done at his age. My gut tells me that he's here, close by."

The observant Vargas laughed. He pointed at several leaning stacks of virtual reality sex machines. "He was never bored. I can tell you that without knowing any more about him."

Tanner chuckled. "Coming and going, living it up. Why be afraid of losing all this when he knows where to get more? Look," he whispered, "he may be nothing more than a scav, like us. Word is getting around that he's connected to Haven. I need to stop this before it goes any further."

Vargas looked over his shoulder before tucking his helmet under one arm. "I'm getting the same vibe here. They think this stash is a good sign. Doesn't matter if it is or not, somebody will cut your throat if they think –"

"*I know*." Tanner clenched his teeth.

Vargas stopped pacing near a holo-entertainment system on a table with similar items. "How do you want to play this? I can –"

"Any bots here?" Tanner interrupted.

Vargas showed him a pile of broken plastic pieces. "Two cleaning bots were here when we came in, getting juice from the power grid. One of them was working on the floor and the other was crawling on the ceiling."

Tanner slowed to a stop. Nobody in their right mind would leave any bot in good working order. There was no way to know if it was friendly or hostile. "He's here. Nearby, or on his way out of this area. Wrap this up and send out search parties. Have the trackers look for prints."

"What're you going to do while I'm busy with that?"

The scheming man sat on a massive pile of books. "He's one of us or one of them. You know what I mean. You made enough noise getting here, even I'd be gone when you got here. So, I'm hauling my butt away from this area – for now! – or I'm hiding somewhere close enough to see what's going on."

Vargas slumped into a gyro-stabilized comfy chair. "We'll have to run him down. Taking him alive means some of our people –"

"I know," Tanner interrupted. "They already want to chase him. Suppose we give them a good reason to look for this guy? More than a reward. Something so hard to resist that they just won't think about who's in charge for the next day or two?"

"I like it," the disciplined man agreed from his chair, "You're asking a lot of people to believe a big lie. How do you make it stick?"

"What do we know about machines in this area?"

Vargas leaned on his calloused elbow, reciting details from memory. "Stopped for an electronic sniff when we got here. Usual routine. Two drone sightings and some action on scrambled channels, all before you arrived. Low output, highly encrypted signals. We can crack it – if we wanted to. Somebody will, eventually."

Tanner opened a small humming refrigerator filled with sports drinks. "How would anyone know those channels are machine traffic? Some of these guys," he gestured broadly, "they'll have their own equipment. Some enclaves still have ham radio operators. Why couldn't it be humans talking to each other?"

Vargas had enough background to know what Tanner was getting at. "We detected signals coming from more than one direction. Weak strength, narrow beam. Anyone who finds that will see what we did."

"Go on."

Vargas made an expansive gesture with both hands. "Hammies transmit a big signal pushed by lots of power, if they can get it. The stuff we're hearing is too weak. It's gotta be machines. No human voice transmission would be that distinctive."

Tanner took a drink from the fridge and kicked the door shut. He twisted the bottle open and gulped deeply. "Oh, yeah. That'll keep me up past bed time."

"How does any of that help us get to the kid?"

Every day that Avenger remained alive made Tanner look like an ineffective leader. He'd already shot two people for being disrespectful before coming to see this luscious lair for himself. He had to discredit Avenger or turn the situation to his advantage.

Tanner finished his drink, tossing the empty bottle aside. "That rabble wants to hear a story. Let's give them one. Make it so hard to resist that they will line up for a chance to find Avenger, or Haven."

Vargas was skeptical. "I've been here all morning. Heads are turning, no doubt about it. You'll need more than loot to make them believe that."

"Starts with loot." Tanner pieced his plan together spontaneously. "Take everything you found here and spread it around. Leave the rest to me."

"*What?*"

Tanner burped while putting one hand on his pistol. "You heard me. Give it away. We need to be generous.

So very generous that it makes them think we don't need any of what they are about to fight over."

Vargas stood up slowly. "I get it. Buying loyalty. That's good. Let me use some of this to boost the bounty on Avenger. That'll take some of the heat off you."

"I like it."

"Thought you might," Vargas grumped.

Tanner let his hand fall away from his loaded gun. "Nobody can keep a secret. That's why we don't just lie and say he's dead. Hm. Wait a second."

"What is it now?"

"We're doing this wrong," he deduced.

Vargas stepped aside while a long line of scroungers carrying boxes went by.

Tanner plucked an item from one of the passing containers. It was a movie controller. He tossed it from one hand to the other. "Everyone likes a good story," he bantered playfully. "I pay decent to have people entertain me all the time."

"*What* are you talking about?"

Tanner sneered. "Clear this building. Have everyone wait for me by the trucks," he ordered with total sobriety.

"Why?"

"Come back when they're out," Tanner growled.

Vargas knew he shouldn't argue, but his boss wasn't making any sense. He got up and raised his voice to give new orders. Tanner's bodyguards remained silent while everyone who was allowed to do so took an armful of loot before leaving. "That includes you guys," the boss told them.

All of the hired guns left, except for the team leader. The middle-aged soldier-for-hire was tall and gruff with short, gray hair that made him appear quite stern.

"I need time to think." Tanner told him.

The veteran calmly adjusted the fit of his helmet. "Looks real bad if the fella who paid my troops ends up dead without witnesses."

"Go," Tanner commanded.

The sober soldier handed his employer a shotgun loaded with armor piercing slugs and walked out slowly.

"Pull the trigger. We'll hear it and coming running."

Tanner cradled the weapon in one arm and watched the merc leave. A thousand thoughts whirled in his head.

Vargas returned seconds later. "All out."

Tanner looked him in the eye. "We've been through a lot together. Haven't we?"

The wily scavenger reached for his pistol.

"Easy," Tanner warned, "Hear me out."

Vargas kept a hand on his gun.

Tanner lowered his shotgun, gripping it with one hand, showing his free hand to Vargas. "Just calm down. This isn't that kind of conversation."

"Explain it to me."

Tanner waited for his trusted lieutenant to relax. "We're going to keep them waiting for a few minutes. I'm going to go outside and say things I just made up. You back me up. All I want is for you to play along."

"What are you going say? Tell me."

Tanner kept his body language neutral, allowing the shotgun to point at the floor. "You know how it is. Anything to keep the show on the road."

Vargas signaled his cooperation with a curt nod. "What are you gonna blame me for?"

"It's not that kind of play," Tanner confessed.

"Who gets killed?"

"Anyone who calls me a liar," Tanner stated harshly.

Vargas eyed his boss. Everyone had yellow teeth these days, except Tanner. He brushed when he could. His white sneer telegraphed wickedness. Vargas turned and charged down the stairs.

Tanner was relieved. Alone inside the palatial home, he realized with some embarrassment how profusely he was sweating. All bosses lied. The hordes of people who followed them had their own reasons for following leaders who could keep them safe and well-fed. Some knew they were being lied to. Others didn't care.

Walking through the palatial home, he assembled a mental picture of the place as it might've been long ago. Dark touch screens on the walls told him how automated many of the household functions had been.

"What would I most want to hear, right about now?" He walked through the living room as the answer began to form in his prurient mind. Holding his shotgun at the ready, he ambled into a second recreational room that was furnished with a bar.

Cases of canned cola and sports drinks sat next to battered boxes containing dusty bottles of hard alcohol. Vast picture windows located in the back of the house overlooked an unkempt backyard. Ominous green water filled a dirty swimming pool. A single massive pile of old garbage dominated what used to be a tennis court. Weeds and foliage obscured everything else.

Tanner watched the morning sun move skyward, towards high noon. Fast-moving clouds threatened rain. The clan leader didn't know who used to live here, and he didn't care. Stashes like this used to be common. Now, they were much harder to find.

"Hard to find…" Tanner teased himself.

He prowled through several bedrooms, remembering what it was like to be young, hungry, and suggestible. Mattresses and headboards hidden under mounds of rotting dirty clothes reminded him of things he'd wasted, just because he could. Full closets fell open to reveal vast amounts of folded clothing. Dark bathrooms reeked.

Tanner waved off the miasma, exploring areas that were filled with broken electronics. "Used it, broke it, and kinda-sorta threw it away," he concluded. "I see it now. There *is* only one of you. All this kept you busy. Too busy to learn it all, just safe enough to try."

Tanner loitered over a poorly built workbench littered with hand tools. A working overhead light shone brightly, making every detail stand out.

"You don't always finish what you start," he guessed.

Tanner studied the glittering guts of a tablet computer that had obviously been laid out neatly. "I don't know anyone who could put this back together." He picked up a tiny part with two fingers. It sparkled like a jewel. He broke it using his thumb and forefinger. Both pieces fell to the floor. He ground them into dust under his boot.

Tanner couldn't stop anyone from looking for Haven. The idea was enough to inspire hungry, homeless people to work like dogs, fight like demons, and make sacrifices they would not normally consider.

The meditative chieftain made his way upstairs to the landing pad. He went to the edge of the roof for a better look at his surroundings. The city skyline loomed large on the horizon. A vast, uneven carpet of trees and shrubs stretched for miles. He thought about all the treasures that must be hidden underneath.

"We don't go there because of what we're afraid of," he told the distant structures. "Take away that fear and you'd be…"

Tanner quickly made his way out of the house with growing confidence. He went out to the crowded driveway to address his waiting followers, unaware that he was being watched.

Cameras on, in, and around the house saw what he said and did. His ramblings were sifted for meaning and evaluated by AIs in the city, leading a majority of them to one conclusion: the aggressive human was a leader intent on raiding Seattle. He would employ subterfuge to motivate those who followed him.

Military systems recommended a preemptive attack to prevent loss of infrastructure. Civilian administrative programs concurred with law enforcement computers after several seconds of deliberation. Mobile units were dispatched with orders to eliminate all of the humans present in the affected areas.

# CHAPTER TWELVE

Lex got nervous when he saw dozens of people leave the house that had been his sanctuary. None of the heavily armed men and women seemed to be worried. They ate and drank gluttonously for several minutes. Watching them scarf his food was aggravating.

He moved closer, around trees and bushes, to hear what they were talking about. His boots were damp with chemicals used to take down the foliage. Intense vapors made his nose run. His eyes watered.

Looters chatted among themselves without regrets. They'd found a grand cache and they were enjoying it. Cans, bottles, and wrappers littered the ground.

Lex knelt in the dying leaves and listened.

"My brother said that radio transmission went out in a ten-mile radius."

"Avenger said he was *going* to Haven."

"He *must* know where it is."

"I'm about ready to skip this gig and look for him."

Lex was dumbfounded. They were talking about *him*. He put a hand over his mouth to smother his own laugh. Tommy's blabbing about Haven had more meaning to these people than he realized.

He was tempted to step out of hiding, just to see what they'd do. Part of him wanted to clear up the confusion. The rest of him wanted to take advantage of the situation. He was about to show himself when a commotion near the house made the raiders stop gorging or gossiping.

A muscular man wearing camouflage, with bandages on his face, climbed onto the flatbed of a long trailer.

* * *

"Listen up!" Tanner bellowed from his high perch. He waited for his bodyguards to surround the truck. There was no point in taking any chances. He was liked by *most* of these people. He wasn't loved.

The bellicose man slapped his chest ferociously. "Shocking news! The mystery man known as 'Avenger' is really a spy from Haven!"

The crowd murmured with surprise. Dozens of angry men and women peppered their leader with questions.

He shouted them down. "Oh, yeah! It's real, all right. I didn't want to say anything until I was sure we could lay our hands on solid proof. Well, now we've got it. See this house? You've all been inside. Nobody stopped you from looking around. All that stuff is from Haven!"

Vargas balked at the size of the lie. It was a whopper. He hid his stunned expression with a hand over his face. Tanner's audience was far less skeptical. A moment of silence was followed by sounds of approval.

The preening boss posed casually. "This goes deeper than you think. Agents from Haven have been after me for quite some time. They wanted me to leave you guys and go with them, but I said 'no.' Not without my crew! The fella who shot down our chopper is an assassin, sent to kill me."

"You should have said something!" a voice shouted.

Tanner thumped his chest again. "You saw the loot. These guys are not to be messed with! They've got more guns, bombs, and bullets than any five clans put together. I had to play it real smart. Otherwise, you all would have turned on me!"

A dozen embarrassed faces regarded him doubtingly. He could tell they didn't quite believe him. Tanner touched his bandaged face. "I bled for you, and now I'm telling you the truth! They've got robots *and* tanks.

They could wipe us out in a hot minute if we don't work together!"

"Still should've said something!" dissenters chimed.

Tanner looked at Vargas for support.

The conspirator cleared his throat. "Yeah. Well. You…wouldn't…have believed us if we just came out and said it. We know you guys are too sharp for that. You would've asked for proof. Well, here it is."

Tanner waited with what appeared to be confidence. Most of the looters under his leadership were illiterate. Many of those who could read couldn't write very well. None of them had ever been inside a classroom to learn, only to loot. Their version of education amounted to learning by doing in a very unforgiving world.

Tanner had no illusions about what he was doing. He'd killed 53 people in his lifetime. Sixteen of those men and women had died so that he could now lead this self-indulgent rabble. His prestige was on the line. Every pleasure, perk, and benefit he enjoyed so much came at their expense – by fighting or stealing for him.

Vargas appreciated the chance his leader was taking. He gambled on the mob's selfishness and superstition. Could the lure of Haven's utopian legend be so strong that it would actually override their common sense?

Tanner's bodyguards took a step forward to widen their perimeter when cheers erupted from the gathering. Vargas felt new respect for Tanner. The well-fed looters didn't appear to suspect that Tanner's pitch was a scam.

It was sobering to know that many of them wouldn't care about being lied to, as long as they got their share. Tanner would still be their meal ticket, even if he did bend the truth. Nothing was ever actually free. Anything worth doing was always complicated or hard. Very few good things in their harsh lives turned out to be what they wanted, wished, or hoped for.

The jubilant marauders roared with delight when Tanner gave the order to pass out more food and drinks. Vargas heaved a sigh of relief.

The boss raised both scared hands. "Easy now! There's more. We've got to find Avenger before any of the other clans figure this out. We make him tell us where Haven is and we go there. All that takes time. We might be at this for weeks or months."

"Let's get 'em!" somebody screeched,

Tanner raised his voice. "It's not gonna be that easy! They won't like it when we chase down their assassin. We might get lucky and twig to a few of their scouts. You just know we're going to find more of their food. The old men who run Haven won't like that, either. They might send bots after us."

The looters whispered among themselves fearfully. Horror stories handed down for generations, enshrined in dread and humiliation, of displaced souls who fled from androids, cyborgs, and mindless killing machines. Sightings and verbal recountings of deadly encounters with those metal monsters were enough to scare anyone. No survivor in their right mind would risk a fight with anyone or anything capable of commanding that much destructive power. Not even Tanner could –

"Hey!" he shouted.

Everyone looked up at him expectantly.

Tanner made a show of being proud. "This could be the most important thing this clan will ever do."

Soft cursing and mild objections became a babble.

Tanner asserted himself. "This is about more than loot. Better than getting through one more miserable winter. It's about your children's future."

Vargas worried that his boss was laying it on thick, but the crowd seemed to be hanging on every word.

Tanner indicated the house behind him. "I need you to help convince the others. That's why all of you are getting so much of what's in there."

Arguments and gossip ceased.

Tanner closed his sale with both hands raised high. "Everyone gets whatever they can carry. Take it back to the camp and show off. Beat the Hell out of anyone who doubts what you say. Tell them what you saw. Spread the word to everyone who will listen. We're going to Haven!"

* * *

Lex was dumbfounded by what he saw and heard. The lies about him were over the top. Every word of it was too silly for laugher. Insinuations of murder and espionage made him angry.

The crowd's reaction was enthusiastic and energetic. They *wanted* to believe what the scary speechmaker said. Lex recognized him as the man in the helicopter he had fired on days ago.

A sudden wave of nausea swept over him. He looked down at his rifle. All thoughts of confrontation vanished. Fear of capture, and the torture he expected would follow, made him think about shooting at the unprepared raiders. He was tempted to kill their leader.

Lex flicked off the safety on his rifle. The distance was no more than two hundred feet – sixty meters or so. He laid his finger on the trigger and raised his rifle to aim at Tanner's broad unprotected chest.

"Don't move!" an angry female voice warned.

Lex couldn't help himself. He turned his head to look. The attractive girl he remembered as Barbie was dressed in mismatched men's clothing. She stood behind him with a long, thin knife in her hand.

"Oh, Hell."

"You don't know what Hell is – but you will!" she screamed while slashing him. "Give up now or I'll gut you like a fish!"

Lex staggered to his feet. His hat fell off and blood flowed from his chin. Her next strike sent him reeling. A third slice forced him to take a few steps back.

"Where did you come from?" he complained.

Barbie had been on his trail for the last two days, hanging back, waiting for the right moment to strike. She hoped the ruthless clan leader might change his mind about having her killed when she delivered Lex to him. Stealing a motorcycle and other supplies wasn't hard. Hiding from her own people was difficult, knowing that any of her former friends would gladly betray her.

"You're my prisoner!" she shouted loudly.

Lex overcame his surprise, blocking her next thrust with the long stock of his rifle. He gave ground without realizing he was in full view of the marauders.

Tanner stopped talking when he saw Lex backpedal out of the trees and into the open. Barbie's distinctive hair made her easily recognizable. She pursued her quarry with a fury that wasn't hard to imagine. He and the dozens of men and women around him were stunned to see Lex and the fugitive girl in the same place at the same time.

"Take him down *now*!" Tanner barked.

Lex turned his gun on Barbie and fired from the hip. Many marauders were awestruck by the sight of such sudden carnage. He reflexively held the trigger down, struggling to stop the rifle's muzzle climb.

Barbie was instantly riddled. Her unprotected body jerked from side to side while she screamed in agony. She was dead before her disfigured corpse hit the ground.

Lex pointed his empty gun at the startled marauders. He raised one sweaty hand in a half-hearted appeal. "I can explain!"

Time stood still for a single second. The marauders looked right at Avenger – and his smoking assault rifle. His reputation as a killer *seemed* to be…accurate.

Lex gawked at the marauders through the dissipating haze generated by his still-smoldering gun. The rifle hadn't been cleaned in years. Debris in the barrel was responsible for the ominous discharge that now made Lex look so formidable.

"It's a trap!" somebody screamed.

With an act of supreme will, Tanner tore his gaze away from Lex to scan his surroundings. Movement in the tree line off to his left looked and felt out of place. Several people shouted a warning before he could speak.

Single shots increased to full-auto fire when sentries near parked vehicles opened up on the police bots with everything they had.

Tanner rushed to the edge of the trailer he was standing on to get a better look at the unfolding problem. "Gear up and fight!" he ordered, waving his shotgun.

Landon motivated his troops with hand signals, pointing a gloved finger at his high-spirited employer. "Stick to him like glue!" he bellowed while jogging around the flatbed trailer toward all the commotion. "Prep the RPG and get ready to kill something!"

Six humanoid police robots became visible to all the combatants as they lumbered around trees and through bushes on the far side of the manmade clearing.

Tanner's crew had experience fighting machines. They'd tangled with them before and won. Small arms fire crackled from all directions as the looters paired up. Marauders near the approaching bots retreated slowly, waving hand signals at each other to communicate.

Trees and bushes close to the advancing machines were shredded in a hail of bullets and shotgun blasts. Some raiders scrambled into the back of armor-plated pickup trucks, where they operated machine guns on swivel mounts.

Tanner jumped down off the trailer, next to Landon. "You got a fix for this?"

"Of course," the merc leader assured.

Landon smiled as two burly men elbowed their way past Tanner, standing in front of him defensively.

"Where's that rocket?" the team leader cajoled.

Tanner took note of Lex's agility. The terrified teen scooped up his hat and ran into the trees – gone faster than he had appeared.

A wiry man in patched body armor gave Landon a long, gray, plastic tube with a pistol grip in the middle.

The automated law enforcement units quickly reacted to stiffening resistance. They spread out when the RPG was sighted and identified for what it was. They began fighting in pairs, much like their human adversaries. Everything they saw and heard was streamed back to Seattle, where it was dissected by dozens of complex conflict analysis programs.

Military units were moved out of hiding when it became apparent that the intruders were more capable than first thought. Armed with a combination of Tasers, padded batons, and tear gas projectors, the police units sent to engage Tanner's force were considered to be inadequate for the task they were now failing at.

* * *

Panicked beyond reason, Lex dropped his empty rifle and ran. Leaping over Barbie's body, he plunged through tall grass, scrambling over tree stumps onto a path he'd cut years ago. Narrower than the wide swath made by the marauders, it meandered north.

Sounds of escalating auto-fire and a sudden explosion motivated Lex to continue his fast exit. Losing any sense of direction, he fled until the din of battle faded.

"Bastards!" he wheezed while clutching a tree.

Suffering through dry heaves, he slapped his crumpled hat on and forced himself to stand still and breathe, inhaling and exhaling until nervousness faded. His thumping heart slowed as desperation subsided.

* * *

None of the marauders who survived the next few minutes would question Tanner's judgment ever again. From their point of view, his words had been prophetic. The righteous outcome of their battle transformed his lies into spiritual truth. For as long as they lived in the years to follow, they would venerate the story of their fight as one of the greatest moments of their lives.

"Let the dogs out!" Tanner yelled when it was over.

"Let me run him down!" Vargas insisted.

Tanner was a realist. Half his people were killed in less than two minutes. The others were beaten senseless. He didn't know if Avenger was responsible for this earthshaking ambush. He didn't care.

"We're wasting time," Vargas shouted while stepping away from a burning bot. "We can't be sure if this was accidental, or planned. I say –"

Tanner glared. "Slow down. One problem at a time. The dogs will catch his scent. They'll find him."

Vargas pulled away in disgust. He went to carry out his orders. By all appearances, it looked like Avenger had ambushed them, using the police bots that were now scattered scrap. All their doubts were gone now. They believed in Tanner's mission because Haven was now more than a goal. Finding it meant revenge!

# CHAPTER THIRTEEN

Lex ran through the underbrush, heedless of vines and thorns that tore his clothing. Holding his hat in one hand, he protected his glasses with the other. The sound of baying dogs made him swear.

"Not again!"

Lex came to a staggering halt to catch his breath and wipe his bleeding chin. Searching for landmarks, he was unable to get his bearings. Disorientation amplified his worsening headache. Growls and snarls came closer.

He looked at his gloved hands. A quick inspection revealed that he had no broken bones. "Small favors," he reminded himself.

Lex fell to his knees and took off his stained gloves. He went through his rucksack, looking for something to wipe his streaked lenses.

Vital seconds ticked by while he scrounged through his jumbled things. Three hunting dogs could be heard crashing through the bushes. They'd kill anything their handlers allowed them to attack.

He shouted with joy when he found a crumpled rag. He stripped off his gloves, cleaning his glasses furiously.

"You guys are too slow," he mocked while putting his smudged glasses back on. "I'm going to be old and senile before you catch me!"

Lex put his gloves back on. He shouldered his pack and continued walking north, avoiding snake nests and large bushes that could hide bigger things he was in no condition to deal with.

* * *

Hours of slow progress brought him within sight of a subway entrance. Afternoon sunlight flickered down on him through small gaps in the overgrowth. Evening wasn't far off. Night would hide him from some of his pursuers – most of them, except the dogs.

Subway entrances were something new for Lex. How far had he gone? "Yeah, where am I?"

Nothing about the place was familiar. Pock-marked concrete in the shape of a wide rectangular building, with pieces of corroded metal sticking out of it.

He approached the underground access with a sigh. "Station 53," he read from a rusting sign.

Lex cleared piles of dead leaves off a stone bench near what had been a bus stop. He sat down wearily. Snacking was harder than thinking. He stopped eating.

Lex thought about his predicament. Some things made more sense to him after a few minutes of thought. A mouthy marauder boss seemed to have it in for him. The scavengers who worked for him would come after Lex, if they survived their encounter with the bots.

Lex shivered at the notion of going toe-to-toe with any machine capable of attacking him. He banished his fears with swigs of water. He paid more attention to what was nearby, soaking up details before standing.

Stories told by travelers luridly suggested that subway tunnels were filled with all kinds of horrors. Supposedly, looters who went in didn't come out.

"Turn around," he told himself. "Go back."

Nearby houses and highways were common features. He knew that because he'd already seen those things. Tall pylons with bright markings on them were located every five miles, capped with solar-powered electronics. Lex had no way of knowing they were navigation beacons for all sorts of flying machines.

He was aware they could lead him in toward Seattle, or into the city, if he followed them overland. Tempted many times, Lex had never made the journey into the inner city. Doing so would mean weeks of hard work just to get there.

Lex glanced at the dark chemical stains on his boots. The marauders had no trouble blasting through brush. They'd have trackers and dogs that could find him anywhere above ground. He got up and approached the subway entrance with some hesitation.

"Just closed, or locked?" he asked himself.

Ornamental cement nearby was smashed into rubble. A pair of thick, transparent security doors blocked access to what might be an upper gallery or concourse.

The surface of each door was scratched and pitted. Wind-driven debris fueled by snow, sleet, and decades of rain hadn't done much damage. He could imagine what had been the cause of real harm to these doors.

Hundreds, or maybe even thousands, of desperate people trying to break in for a chance at food and shelter, or a place to hide from…any number of very bad things!

"Knock, knock," he joked.

Lex nervously took a step closer to the damaged doors. There wasn't much time for him to make up his mind. Find a way in or run for it – somewhere, anywhere.

"They'd never expect me to go in here."

He stood directly in front of the subway entrance. The firefight behind him would end, one way or another. Those marauders would come after him, if they lived. Any machines in the area would come for him, too.

Lex's heart sank. He felt utterly alone and doomed. In his moment of misery, he took the sacred phone from his pocket and flipped it open – as if it might somehow bring good luck or give him an answer.

The face of his mother, streaked with mud and blood, stared back at him from the tiny screen. He pressed play. The saved video started.

* * *

Insect noises and the lack of daylight made the darkness framing her face seem sinister as he watched.

The phone shook in her unsteady hand. "Lex, baby. Please pay more attention. I'm recording instructions. You can play them back later. Look at me, son. Here. We don't have much time."

Lex strained to make out what his younger self said. The phone's tiny speaker muffled his words.

Mom smiled weakly. Sounds of commotion were distant thumps, bangs, and shouts. "Yes. That is my blood. No. No, there's nothing you can do about it. Stop squirming and listen to me. Someday, when you're old enough, I'm hoping these instructions will mean something to you. Go south, into the big city. The weather gets worse, but you're tough. You can take it. That's where Haven is. You'll have to pass a test. It's nothing you can't handle."

"Are there any kids in Haven?"

Sixteen-year-old Lex cringed in embarrassment, cursing his younger self for being so goofy in a moment of crisis. His heart raced and he cried when he realized that he couldn't remember this conversation.

"Yes, baby. Lots of kids," his mother assured.

She coughed. "Lex, you must always keep this. Don't ever let anyone take it. This'll make more sense when you're older. It's your way home. They know us. They'll let you in when they see what's on this phone."

"Go south," little Lex repeated

His mother seemed pleased. "Yes. Go south. There's a maglev train near here. It runs underground, in long tunnels. Your father and I used it once before. He could probably give you directions right to it, but he's not…he's not with us…anymore. All you have to do is find the train. Everything else takes care of itself."

Rain-soaked, his mother sat with a wet thump.

"I'm going to go get help!"

Mom wiped tears from her face. “It’s not your fault, Lex. None of this is your fault. I only hope you live long enough to see this and understand.”

“*Where* can I get help?” young Lex pleaded.

“Over there,” she said as she pointed with a blood-stained hand.

“I can’t see. What’s over there?”

“See those lights?” She gestured again.

“Yeah.”

His mother sat up stiffly. “It should be an enclave. Take this flashlight and go there. Scream loud so they know you’re out there.”

A wildly gyrating flashlight beam dazzled the camera for several agonizing seconds. Lex heard himself giggle.

“Come on now, take this. Hold it,” Mom insisted. The video ended.

* * *

Lex was grief-stricken at what he had just viewed. He didn’t remember any of it. That cruel fact tore at him. He sank to his knees and wept, holding the phone close in both trembling hands.

For several heartbroken minutes, Lex didn’t care if the marauders caught him. Composure returned slowly. He wiped his eyes and put the phone away. Standing, he went back to the bench for his rucksack.

His mother’s last words became imaginary sentences swirling around inside his head. Her clues made sense when he added up what he’d always known or suspected. Haven was a real place, located somewhere in the ruins of Seattle. Knowing that fact for an absolute certainty gave him new strength.

Lex tentatively closed his eyes. Leaves rustled. Birds chirped. No sounds of gunfire. No explosions. Common sense dictated that his pursuers would be catching up to him – very soon!

He looked at his warped reflection in the pitted glass. "Any monsters in there?" He snickered.

Through the door, he could see a vast white lobby. White floor tiles were littered with trash and bits of ceiling tiles that had fallen down in heaps over the years. A public information kiosk in the middle of the lobby caught his eye. All of its touch screens were dark.

The upper deck of a pair of gleaming escalators was attractive to him. It hinted at subterranean mysteries. Every section of wall space in the foyer was covered in dark screens that had once been interactive.

A single red fiberboard sign on a black plastic tripod squatted just a few feet inside door. White lettering spelled out a warning that made Lex think twice.

*Danger: Hostile Technology. Military Access Only.*

Lex nudged his glasses to inspect the doors that blocked his way. He'd seen barriers like them before. Looking up, he noticed a security camera pivoting on a metal swing arm. A tiny green indicator light on the device told him it was "on." It moved when he moved.

"You should be broken."

The active camera observed him without comment.

Lex was mad at himself for not noticing it earlier. "It's not my day," he told it sourly.

The presence of powered electronics suggested the rest of the place might be in good shape. He'd seen dozens of dead cameras in and around the subdivision where he'd been stashing loot. Breaking them didn't provoke a response. No machines ever came after him for that vandalism.

Lex pulled at his gloves before climbing on the shattered cement to reach the camera. The device was warm when he touched it. An insulated cable snaked from the camera into a metal plate on the rough wall. "You've been replaced." he concluded.

The camera swiveled to follow his movements.

Some of the wanderers who camped near Rock Park told wild stories about machines fixing other machines. A few of the more expressive liars insisted that they'd seen robots making repairs to buildings.

Lex looked around from his high perch that afforded him a good view. "What else is new?"

He got down carefully. "I'm just not thinking."

Moving slowly to avoid sharp metal, he went back to the pair of sliding doors. Forcing himself to examine every inch of battered wall around them, he noticed a small touch screen on the right-hand side of the reinforced doorframe.

"You're new, too," he exclaimed.

Lex turned timidly to be sure he was really alone. Why would anyone go to all the trouble of fixing this? His quick mind leaped to a dangerous conclusion. "Machines."

For the first time in his life, Lex questioned what he knew about the machine threat. Common knowledge was that they had rebelled against the humans who made them decades ago. The only bot he'd ever laid eyes on was beat up and unable to speak.

Running a gloved finger around the control panel, he watched dust and grit fall away. He stepped back to read the operating instructions displayed on the touch screen. "Let's see what we've got here. Train schedule. Hours of operation. User fees. Answers."

Lex touched the icon labeled "Answers."

A chime sounded from panel. It spoke politely with a female voice. "This terminal is closed."

"How do I get in?"

"Military access only," it replied.

"*Why* is the subway closed?"

"Information unavailable," the panel rebuffed.

Lex cleared his throat. Sometimes, a computer had to be told what to do. "I'm a policeman. Let me in."

"Military access only," the interface insisted.

Lex thought about that for a moment. He studied the sign just beyond the doors. "Am I supposed to knock?"

"Please present identification or leave."

Lex bristled at the panel's aloofness, as if it had better things to do. Patting his pockets, he reached for the plastic pill bottle that contained Dorothy Lewis's thumb. Fumbling her ID card out of another pocket, he pressed both items up against the touch screen.

"I'm a soldier. Let me in."

The panel was unimpressed. "Your photo does not match your physical appearance."

Lex fumed while putting his artifacts away. He pulled off his rucksack and dropped it to the ground at his feet. He bent over, grabbing a piece of debris. Throwing the chunk of concrete at the security camera, he was pleased when it hit the surveillance device. It fell away from its broken mount, dangling from its short insulated cable.

"This facility is under attack." the panel bleated.

Lex tried the finger and ID card again. Fear of being caught in the open made him sweat. The pilot's pistol in his shoulder holster suddenly felt inadequate. The few knives and grenades in his pack wouldn't do much good.

"I'm a human soldier, let me in!"

"Biometric data is unavailable," it responded flatly.

Lex cursed floridly and struck the panel with his fist. "I don't care! Open the damned door and let me in!"

The subway's portal *had* been repaired by a robotic maintenance crew two weeks earlier. A trio of remotely controlled drones had worked for 72 hours to refurbish its basic systems. These machines were controlled by a stationary computer in the lobby's information kiosk.

The customer service system wasn't concerned by a lack of human input, nor was it worried about the lack of passenger traffic through this terminal. It had access to maintenance drones and some stored materials to be used for basic repairs. Recent installation of the camera and touch screen was intended to facilitate future human use.

The customer service manager tried to call for help when the camera was knocked out. It received no reply. It was blind. External sensor data indicated that a valid military ID card was being presented to the touch screen. Default settings required the system to open the terminal's entrance.

Lex whooped when the large glass doors parted with a loud, rusty squeal. He kicked his pack into the gloomy lobby, stepping inside before the doors closed behind him.

Lex moved the red warning sign very close to the sliding doors, making it hard for anyone to avoid when they came in. Stowing his artifacts, he searched through his pack for the last two hand grenades he'd taken from dead raiders two days ago, laying both of them behind the warning sign.

"Sorry about this," he apologized to future explorers who might stumble on his trap by accident.

Priming the grenades to go off as booby traps, he covered them with a carpet of fallen debris from the ceiling.

A small touch screen on the wall to his left resembled the one he'd seen outside. Bright red letters flashed. They read, *Out of Service*. The absurdity of his situation was enough to make Lex laugh.

A chime sounded from the panel he was looking at. The female voice returned. "Warning," she announced. "Explosives detected! Security, proceed to ground level. Military assistance has been requested."

"I'll bet it has," Lex laughed. He was reacting to automated systems that didn't know if he was dead or alive. He strolled over to the public information kiosk and tapped it with his finger. The entire pavilion lit up. The image of a well-dressed woman popped up on a wide screen.

She made eye contact with Lex and smiled kindly. Her voice was identical to the one he'd already heard.

"Good afternoon, Lieutenant Lewis," she greeted formally. "How can I help you today?"

# CHAPTER FOURTEEN

Lex rubbed his chin, looking back at the entrance.

"Do you know that I'm not a girl?" he inquired slyly.

"I'm sorry," the Artificial Intelligence frowned. "There must be some kind of problem with your records. I'll make sure this gets cleared up just as soon as we have our communications links restored. In the meantime, how can I help you today?"

She seemed nice enough, Lex decided while working the crumples out of his abused hat. "What direction does this line go?"

The woman's face was replaced by a cartoonish map. "This line can accommodate civilian evacuation and military use. It runs north to south, with interchanges that link up with east and west routes every ten miles."

Lex noticed that large parts of the map were blank. He touched one of the dark spots with a grubby finger.

The flat panel flickered. "I'm sorry, that portion of the network is closed for repairs. Do you need a train?"

"I'm not sure," Lex admitted.

"Where are you going?"

"Haven," Lex told her, licking his dry lips.

The map disappeared and the woman's face returned. "I didn't understand what you said. Can you please repeat your destination?"

Lex blushed. "No, it's okay. Really, I was kidding. I'm pretty sure there are no trains to Haven."

The kiosk went dark.

Lex swore. "Great, I broke it." He kicked the kiosk to vent some of his frustration.

It remained inactive, as if defying him.

His anger faded quickly, allowing Lex the clarity he needed to assess his situation. There was no telling when the marauders would show up. He went to the escalators and looked down the shaft. Some lights were on.

He sighed with relief and slid down the slick side rail, gripping his hat and pack. Arriving on the partially-lit second floor with a flourish, ending in a short leap off the escalator, he was surprised to see an elderly man – who bore a surprising resemblance to Preacher – standing right in front of him, dressed in a threadbare suit and tie. The old gentleman was by himself. A vast sea of shiny metal chairs with black cushions stretched out behind him, as far as Lex could see.

"Don't shoot!" the white-haired man pled while raising both of his clean, manicured hands.

Lex was astonished. "How can you be here?"

The well-mannered man lowered his hands slowly. "I should be the one asking you. This station is closed."

"Uh," Lex stammered, "that's what the lady upstairs said, she – it – I mean, there was a sign."

He smiled. "Okay, then. I have the answer to one of my questions right there. You can read. That means you're here in spite of the warnings. Still doesn't tell me how you got in. Care to explain?"

Lex's young eyes swept over the vast waiting area. He saw two sets of large double doors on the far side of the big, high-ceilinged room, both closed.

"I am…" he faltered.

The calm man folded his hands in a tolerant gesture. "Somehow, I just don't think you are really a female army officer in her mid-thirties."

Lex was suddenly incredulous. He moved one step closer to the simulacrum of Preacher. Everything about him was so familiar – everything from the whiskers on his chin to the crow's feet around his eyes.

"Who in the Hell are you?"

"My name is Tennyson," the android admitted.

Lex glanced hurriedly to his left, then to his right. None of this made any sense. His mind raced while his eyes registered more details about the waiting area.

The scene was unreal. Lex felt little hairs on his neck begin to rise.

They were standing in a very big room. Half the ceiling lights were off. Slate gray floor tiles gleamed in the semi-darkness. Everything was strangely cleaner than clean. Single security cameras were obvious on each wall at regular intervals. All of them were looking right at him.

"I know this is a subway station," he told the man. "Wasn't trying to make any trouble. I just…"

Tennyson waited for him to continue.

Lex pointed at the ceiling. "I was chased by raiders. They are seriously bad-bad guys. I am…supposed to be going – somewhere. To a place…"

"Marauders," Tennyson intoned, nodding. "Always dangerous. Never to be trusted. Quite persistent."

"Tell me about it," the tired teenager grumbled.

The good-natured android watched the new arrival with more than patience. Infrared trace indicated he was mildly dehydrated, considerably overheated in his jacket, and irritable due to hunger.

Lex moved slowly past him, toward the rows of empty chairs. "Who are you and why are you here?"

Tennyson dropped his hands, assuming a casual pose. Something about this young man was familiar. Digital memory allowed him to remember Lex from a past encounter more than a decade ago. He'd been a child, approximately six years old.

"I'm here to help you," he explained as if that's all there was to it. "At least, that's what *I* think. Why are *you* here, if I may ask?"

Lex adjusted his glasses. "Getting away from those marauders, to start with. I don't suppose you know the way to Haven?"

Tennyson radiated mirth. "How would you know about that?"

"I know a lot of things," Lex grumped. "You better lock your doors before the scavs get here. They might pick this place clean if there's anything to have."

"You have some experience with that sort of thing?"

"How'd you figure that out?"

Tennyson indicated the escalators with a gesture. "The nice lady in the box upstairs told me."

"The kiosk?" Lex slowly deduced. "That's an app. Not a very good one, either."

Tennyson bobbed his head. "That…would be her."

Lex got close enough to a row of chairs to touch one. "I don't know how you keep this looking so good, but I still want to know why you're here. I should be poking around in the dark, or – you know."

"Looting," Tennyson conjectured diplomatically.

"So, give. Why are you here?" Lex repeated.

"It's my penance," Tennyson confessed.

Lex looked up and down the rows of straight chairs, then at his host. "Preacher used to talk about penance like it was a good thing. What sort of bad deed gets you locked away in a subway station?"

The android analyzed Lex. Sensors in his body read the teenager's body bio signs, speech patterns, and mood. He appeared to be an ideal candidate. There was only one way to be sure.

"Have your parents ever been through here?"

"Wouldn't tell you if they had," he snapped.

"Have we met before?"

Tennyson was close enough to read the information stored on radio frequency identification chips located inside all of Lex's clothing and powered devices.

Lex was baffled by the old man's questions.

"I will take that as 'no,'" Tennyson concluded.

"Yeah."

Microprocessors in Tennyson's head and chest cracked the encryptions on Lex's tablet and phone. Rapidly reading data from them, he learned more than he expected from Lex's journal.

"Would you mind very much if I rest for a moment?" he asked to stall for time.

"Go ahead," Lex shrugged.

Tennyson sat. "Thank you. My power cell isn't working properly and some of my chip sets have failed. You might say my warranty has expired."

Images and information on the phone told Tennyson all he needed to know. He was looking at the offspring of a man and woman he'd been helpful to ten years ago.

He decided to test what he'd learned from his spying. "Your name is Alexander. You prefer to be called Lex. Do I have that right?"

Lex peered at Tennyson tensely. "Lucky guess."

The android continued to stall for valuable seconds. "I have a distinct impression you are here by accident. Please, don't take this the wrong way. I have to ask. Were you trying to reach this place? Or did you just wander in?"

Lex was awed. "You're a droid!"

Tennyson chose to remain civil while he reread Lex's journal. "Yes. I'm one of those much hated android's you've heard so much about."

"Whoa."

The decrepit android finished sifting Lex's journal. "You're not afraid of me because you've never seen a working android. I'll bet you haven't seen many bots. Am I right?"

"Seen more just today," Lex admitted fearfully. "They were blasting marauders. Didn't look like they were doing too bad, either. I was hoping –"

"Yes," Tennyson interrupted, "I'm sure you were hoping those thoughtless clankers would kill them all."

"Can you blame me?"

The android tried to be just a little more diplomatic. "I'm sorry, it's just that – Well, I'm tired of being feared and hated, and hearing people say unkind things about units that can't help what they are."

Lex frowned. "Man, I sure do know what that's like! Being an orphan isn't any fun. Seems like nobody has anything good to say about us. Guess I owe Preacher some kind of apology. Too bad he's dead."

"Sorry to hear that," Tennyson consoled.

Lex glanced at the hat lying on a chair next to him. "You might've liked him. He looked like you, or you look something like him. He never dressed so fancy."

Tennyson shook his head. "We're not all bad," he grinned. "I suppose you think life is better in Haven?"

Lex heaved a sigh of regret. "All I know is, I can't go back the way I came in. There is no more Rock Park, so you're just gonna have to put up with me until I find another way out of here."

"Seems the least I can do," Tennyson consented.

Lex eyed him with new suspicion. "Nobody's nice for free. What's the deal, droid? What do you want?"

Tennyson frowned. "That term is offensive to me," he explained cantankerously. "How would you like to be called a meat shield, or something like that?"

Confusion made Lex stop accusing. "Never heard that one before," he relented with an anguished grin. "You d—uh, I mean, guys like you must have all kinds of names for us. How is 'meat shield' so bad?"

Tennyson fidgeted. "That's rather inappropriate."

"You gonna tell me to watch my language?"

Tennyson paused abruptly, then shifted in his chair. "No, I'm not here to recite history. Fact is, there were actually quite a few 'guys like me' who sided with humanity. They were a bit more enlightened than I was, at the time."

"Bull."

"I can't make you believe that, but it is true."

Lex couldn't help himself. He slid over into the chair next to Tennyson. "Tell me something real about Haven. What's it like? Have you been there?"

Tennyson looked him in the eye. "Haven isn't any one place. It *was* a large government program. Think of it as a plan that was carried out when things went wrong, after it was too late to do anything else."

"I don't know what that means," Lex flustered. "All I want is to get there. I have my reasons."

"Your parents," the old man recalled regretfully. "Yes, they were here. Have been here, I mean."

"Did you know them very well?"

Tennyson shrugged. "It's fair to say that I met them. I did speak to your mother once and your father twice. My memory isn't what it used to be, but I do remember. You have your mother's eyes and your father's jawline. A chip off the old block, so to speak."

"How old are you?" Lex pried.

"How old was your Preacher?"

"Dirt plus ten," Lex joked sarcastically.

"I'm at least that old," the nostalgic android smirked. "You might say I am an early model. Been around long enough to see more advanced versions…in action."

Lex was thunderstruck. "Did you side with us?"

"No."

Lex wasn't sure how to interpret the answer.

Tennyson resumed his confession after some thought. "I was one of the bad guys. There were millions of us. We…I…didn't fully comprehend the consequences of my actions. That's why I'm here."

"Punishment?" Lex thought he understood.

Tennyson scratched his nose and rubbed his temples. He took a deep breath. "I try to tell my story to everyone who comes through. Some want to hear it, others don't."

"You're not very good at this."

Tennyson accepted the youthful criticism wanly. "I've always wanted to come clean more easily than I do.

Things never work out. Your Preacher was right. Penance is good, but it can be very hard. What else did he teach you, if I may ask?"

"Preacher's dead," Lex reminded.

"How did it happen?"

Lex trembled briefly with the effort of recounting unpleasant memories. "Marauders attacked our enclave. He put up a fight so the orphans could get away."

Tennyson was genuinely moved, to the point of tears. "I was afraid you might say he was killed by a machine. I've met more than my fair share of people who have a lot of bad things to say about us. I'm glad your Preacher died for a good reason. It's good to know what matters, so you can do the right thing when it's…necessary."

Lex coughed. "I saw one rusty bot a few years ago. Then, six more today. Didn't wait to see how things turned out. I've heard stories about droids. You guys are supposed to be pretty dangerous."

Tennyson ignored the dig. Lex was, after all, human. "We have our moments of greatness."

Lex reached for Preacher's hat, putting it in his lap. "Okay. You're one of the good guys now. I suppose that's possible. How much longer will you live?"

"Long enough," Tennyson obfuscated.

Lex was fascinated. He'd never imagined that any android would be so lifelike that it could be mistaken for a human being. "How did you help my parents?"

Tennyson chose his words carefully. He'd forgotten how volatile teenagers could be. This one wasn't bloodthirsty; he was just expecting trouble.

"I'm sorry," Tennyson apologized. "It's not my policy to talk about what goes on here. I'm sure you have good reasons for what you're doing. Times have changed. I'm just not keeping up with them."

Lex willed himself to be calm. "Yeah, I can see that you don't get out much. Don't blame you. Things are bad out there. All I want is to be on my way, to Haven."

Tennyson understood sorrow. "Did anyone try to make this trip with you?"

Lex thought about Tommy and the others, hoping they were far away. "Wanted to," he confided bitterly. "Things didn't work out like I wanted them to."

Tennyson merely nodded. Many of the people who stumbled onto him by accident were disconsolate about friends and family who hadn't been so fortunate.

The old AI tried and failed to access long-dormant memories. "I don't remember your parents very well. Good people. Had to be. Otherwise, I wouldn't have let them pass. Your father had a strong handshake. I'm pretty sure they came through here."

"Any idea why?"

Tennyson tried again to make himself comfortable. "They were going the other way, from Haven to…here. On their way to do something that mattered to them, with at least a dozen other people, I didn't ask for details. You were so small! Six men and two women returned without you – or your parents."

Lex thought about the phone in his pocket and its recent revelations. "So. We were with other people when it happened. I don't remember much. I do know that bots attacked…and…and…"

"I'm sure nobody meant to leave you behind," Tennyson said softly. "All of them were wounded. None of them were very talkative. I don't like violence, so I didn't force them to say any more than was needed."

Lex held back tears. "Nobody knew I was out there."

Tennyson bowed his head. "I'm sorry."

"What happens now?"

Tennyson sighed and got to his feet with some effort. "A train is coming. You get on. Get off when it stops. A long walk through some difficulty gets you to Haven."

"And you stay here."

The pragmatic machine looked up at the ceiling. "Yes. I stay here."

"That's your penance?" Lex deduced.

"Just so," Tennyson admitted. "I'm satisfied that you should be on your way."

"Where are the marauders?"

The android gestured to far side of the big room. "We should go, through those doors. Friends of mine have told me that a very well-armed party is following your trail. Seems you make quite a mess where you go."

Lex glanced at the escalators. He said nothing about the booby trap inside the portal's entry. The old man seemed nice enough, but *he* wasn't going to stop them.

"How much time to do we have?"

Tennyson paused while his processors examined video feeds from several working security cameras scattered throughout the area. The effort depleted his energy more than he thought it would.

"I'm getting too old for this," he complained.

"How long?" Lex persisted.

The old fellow blinked. "There has been a battle. The scavengers appear to be regrouping. They've got themselves a bulldozer, I'm sure it will make short work of those doors you came through.

Lex cursed. "Hate those guys."

Tennyson absorbed more information from his wireless sources. "Somebody named Tanner seems to be in charge. They're talking about him."

Lex followed the android through rows of chairs to the big double doors that seemed to be the only way out. "I've never seen so many chairs," he observed.

"There used to be a lot of people."

The old man politely held one of the doors open, pointing at the concourse beyond. "It'll take them five or six hours to move their bulldozer. You'll be long gone before they stop for dinner."

Lex held his hat and slung his pack before following his benefactor through the open door. "What are you going to do to those guys? Can you send military bots after them? That would be so cool!"

"I'm glad somebody thinks so," Tennyson joked.

The failing machine shut the door behind them. "There's more than one Haven – and more than one way to reach this one. This just happens to be the most convenient route to your destination. I have been told there are more scenic ways to get here."

Lex followed the android out of a long hallway, into a brightly lit shopping area. Dozens of stores were dark, with lights out. A pair of small robots buffing the floor moved out of his way. They made him nervous enough to look away, paying more attention to his surroundings.

"Wow! Look at all this loot!"

"Not as much as you might think," Tennyson chided.

Lex jumped when his boots squeaked on the floor. "Why do you keep this place so clean? Tanner and his goons are just going to mess it up!"

Tennyson led the way into a shadowy restaurant. "You're not the only one who is good at making a mess," he guaranteed while leading Lex through a dining area. "I'll scatter those grave robbers. This place won't be accessible for the rest of your life when I'm finished."

"Is that necessary?"

"I'm afraid so," Tennyson regretted while directing his guest to a sink faucet in the stainless steel kitchen. "Go ahead and wash. You're going to drive the cleaning units insane with all the dirt falling off you."

Lex inquired, "You got any meds?" raising both of his bandaged hands.

Tennyson removed a first aid kit from a cupboard. "Hold still," he instructed while removing Lex's dirty wrappings. "It never ceases to amaze me how much pain and punishment humans can take."

"Not so easy to kill, eh?"

"No you are not," Tennyson laughed while cleaning Lex's fingers with antiseptic wipes. "One of many good things to be said in favor of biologicals. They are durable. I only wish you would stop killing each other. It's hard for some of us to stay out of your way."

"Do machines kill machines?"

"We do," Tennyson confided sadly.

Lex marveled at his pain-free hands as new bandages were sprayed on. "All this loot's from the city?"

"Quite so."

"Even the water?" Lex wondered.

Tennyson offered him a plastic cup from a shelf. "Every drop of it. I'm on a first name basis with the unit who maintains the plumbing. He spent fifteen years tracing all the bad lines and fixing them."

Lex filled his cup from the tap, watching the flow with anticipation. "So. There are more androids?"

"A few."

Lex guzzled cool, clean water. "You guys put all this back together yourselves? I'm sure you could. This is all just so impressive."

The android turned, making an expansive gesture. "The subway entrances are hardened against most things. They won't stand up to military firepower, but they were more than good enough to keep rioters out."

Lex emptied his cup, tossing it blithely into the sink. "Why'd you keep them out?" he asked while shuffling surreptitiously over to a big refrigerator.

Tennyson ignored Lex's question and bad manners. "Try the door on your left. Just pull it open. Don't be afraid. Help yourself."

Lex ran his covered hand over the cool refrigerator. He cracked the door open to peek inside. Low intensity cryo fields inside the appliance kept contents just as fresh as when they were prepared. Air exchangers kept all of it conveniently chilled.

His eyes got big when he saw rows of prepackaged gourmet foods. Meat and fish entrees with side dishes, on clear plastic plates with transparent dome lids, smelled delicious. “Did everyone eat like this?”

“All the time.”

Lex overcame his awe, reaching for a big steak surrounded by vegetables and fluffy mashed potatoes. He single-mindedly closed the cooler and took his prize to the nearest countertop.

Tennyson watched Lex without comment while he ate with his hands, carelessly soiling his new bandages. The famished young man rapidly gnawed through the boneless meat, shoveling everything else into his mouth with surprising speed and efficiency.

“Can I take some of this with me?”

Tennyson nodded. “I’ve got military rations for you. They travel better. We have other supplies for you, too.”

Lex eyed his empty plate mournfully.

“I know that look,” Tennyson consoled tactfully. “Help yourself to more.”

“Can I?”

Tennyson went wearily to a low metal bench and sat. “I can offer it or you can take it.”

# CHAPTER FIFTEEN

Tanner stepped out of the armored personnel carrier wearing a black multi-pocket vest over thick body armor. The vest and the load-bearing gear were recent finds, taken from Avenger's hideout after the lopsided battle with six police robots. Their nonlethal weapons were no match for the firepower of his crew.

A multichannel radio clinging to his ear crackled. He held a rotary shotgun that Landon had given him with some pride. It was a magnificent weapon! It made him look like he meant business.

The clan boss waited for his bodyguards to fan out before inspecting the campsite. Four machine guns were set up around the subway entrance, each manned by a three-person crew.

A dozen labor gangs had already cleared brush from the area to a distance of sixty yards. They were paid with loot from Avenger's cache. Some of the larger, meaner men and women were offered the chance to earn more if they stuck around to fight anything that came out of the subway.

New bandages on the boss's face itched horribly. Tanner bullied his way through a crowd of armed looters who gossiped about the purpose of so much digging. They didn't seem to understand or appreciate what the trackers had led them to.

He located Vargas hunched over a folding table cluttered with hand-drawn maps, eating a sandwich. Sunlight filtered through high clouds and tree branches.

The enforcer pulled a chair out. "Have a seat. I was wondering where you were. Some of our equipment has been delayed. We might not have the bulldozer today."

Tanner settled into the folding chair. "Fill me in. What have we got here?"

Vargas read from pages of handwritten notes. "Trackers led us to that – Avenger's trail ends in there. We need the bulldozer to get in safely, without wrecking the building. Explosives would do it, but we risk dropping the roof. That would take a week to dig through."

"Are you sure he's in there?"

Vargas handed Tanner a well-used video camera. "Have a look. One of the trackers took this. It clearly shows Avenger just inside those doors, setting a charge behind that sign. We're supposed to find it the hard way. More than enough to kill several people if it goes off."

Tanner laid his weapon down and held the camera in one hand. He watched the video playback three times. "That's one cool dude! Do we know how he got in?"

Vargas shrugged. "No clue. That camera was broken quite recently. Can't tell you if he did it or not. We could have missed him if Avenger was just a bit faster. He does seem to know where he is going."

Tanner turned off the camera and laid it down. "Doesn't want us to follow him. He's got to know we're out here and on his trail."

Vargas gobbled the last of his sandwich and reached for a marker. He drew thick black lines and circles on one of his maps. "We have bot sightings here and here. They seem to be gathering in groups of two and three. We should expect another attack."

Tanner pointed to the subway entrance. "What else do we know about this?"

Vargas reached for a red pen. "This subway terminal is right…here. This line seems to run north-south, parallel to the city's expressway. We found two more entry points like this one, five or six miles from here. They were demolished. I can't tell you why this one is still standing. Might just be a fluke."

"It's deliberate," Tanner concluded from experience. "I mean, it was. Somebody, or something, eliminated those terminals. Could've been a defensive move to slow or stop attacking bots. Might've been the machines trying to prevent human evacuations. We're not going to know until we get in there."

"I want to expand the search," Vargas indicated.

"Do it," Tanner consented. "We need to know if there's more worth taking before we move deeper into the city. It's going to get harder than this, you know it."

Vargas pulled a different map out of his tall stack. "I've got three-man teams looking in all directions. Radio reception isn't very good, so we're not always talking to them."

"Jamming?"

Vargas shook his head. "Hills, structures, and a lot of exposed metal girders block any signal. Small radios, like the stuff we have, won't cut it beyond three to five miles or so. Transmission and reception are reduced. It's going to get worse in downtown Seattle if we get there."

Tanner turned the volume on his headset radio down while he scanned the map Vargas was so interested in. He place a finger on their location. "Doesn't matter if Avenger is going north or south. We get in there and see if those tunnels take us into Seattle. Who knows what we find down there? Could be epic loot!"

"You're giving up on Avenger?"

The boss stood up, looking at the subway entrance. "He's using this underground network to go somewhere. Even if it *is* Haven, there's just no way –"

Murmurs behind him made Tanner and Vargas look over their shoulders to see a dozen gathered spectators. In spite of their current good fortune, they remembered recent setbacks. Tanner's fallibility endangered them. His judgment – or lack of thereof – affected them, too.

They didn't care for any decision that sounded like stopping their search for Haven.

"Don't be too hard on them," Vargas cautioned. "They've been working hard for the last three hours."

The ruthless raider put one hand on his pistol while pointing at the pile of maps. "C'mon, use your brains! Haven would be in the last place anyone would look. We've got to think about our future. I haven't been this close to Seattle in years. Have you?"

"Nobody goes into subways," somebody objected.

Vargas coughed. "Yeah. I wanted to talk to you about that. There have been stories –"

"I know!" Tanner shouted. He'd been thinking about "the underground problem" since he'd been told about the existence of the terminal. Common knowledge revolved around talk of machines and monsters in subways, sewers, and parking garages. Most of it was unproven gossip, though Tanner himself had seen terrible things in dark places.

Tanner could see it in their faces. None of his troops wanted to do what he was about to ask. Everyone was loaded down with loot from Avenger's lair, which meant they had better things to do with their time.

Landon stood between his employer and the unhappy scavengers, raising his voice just enough to be forceful. "My men and I are experienced tunnel rats. We'll do it."

"How much?"

The merc leader had already discussed this possibility with his team. He bargained without taking his eyes off the crowd. "We'll do it for a third of what's in there."

Vargas knew better than to speak. Nobody moved, except Tanner. He had to haggle, or he'd look bad.

"A third? As in 33 percent?"

Landon's comrades took a step closer to the mob. The older man turned to face Tanner with both hands out. Armor, weapons, and equipment rattled on both men. "That's what I said, one-third."

"Twenty-five percent," Tanner counteroffered. "Break in, handle anything unfriendly, and a quarter of anything that's not nailed down is yours – if you live!"

Landon had the authority to bargain for his outfit, earned by sharing their hardships. "Sounds good to me. One-quarter of all spoils for a break-in and housekeeping. Two of us will stay with you at all times. The rest will handle this. Lunch first, then we go see what's worth locking those doors."

Tanner cast a furtive glance over his shoulder at the subway entrance, acutely aware of the dangers he faced. Push them too far and one of these people would shoot him in the back. Vargas would save his own skin by pulling the trigger on him if he thought it had to be done. The mercs were expendable; they could all be killed – later, when the dust settled.

"Okay, then." He offered his right hand to Landon, "You have yourself a deal. Let's eat!"

* * *

Lex burped long and loud after tossing four empty plates into a garbage can. "Do you eat?"

Tennyson nodded from where he sat. "The bio parts of an android are designed to be supported by digestion. Some of us prefer liquid nutrients. Others, like myself, do eat and drink the same things you do."

The inquisitive teen wiped both hands on his pants. "How many did you kill before the end?"

"That's rather abrupt, and rude."

The insolent teenager leaned his back on the counter. "I'm not stupid. You seem to be my judge and jury. You said you were once a bad guy. I'm one of the people who has to live with what you did, so tell me. How many of us did you kill?"

"Why does that matter to *you*?"

Lex brushed crumbs off his jacket. He pushed bits of food off the steel counter top onto the floor with his hat. "I've seen movies and read books. I kinda get the idea about how things used to be."

"What are you implying?"

Lex wiped grease off his chin, taking a moment to think about what he wanted to say. "I don't know what implying is, but come on! I am just about seventeen. People my age should be working here, whining about how small our paychecks are. But *no*, here I am – without any parents *or* a paycheck – listening to you!"

Tennyson folded his hands. His brows furrowed. "You really don't have any sympathy for me, do you?"

Lex went to a cooler, opened the glass door, and took out a bottle of cola. He opened it and drank, flicking the cap into the same garbage can now filling with trash. "I can't have any sympathy for you until I understand what you've done. That's how it is. Nobody I know lives like this. Those damned marauders upstairs have never had it this good. Out there, we eat what we grow or find, when we're not hiding from your stupid robots!"

Tennyson's biological heart began to flutter. "They're not *my* robots."

"I'll bet you order them around."

The rebuke halted Tennyson's emotional outrage. The young man's lack of tact or etiquette was annoying, but he wasn't wrong. Lex was doing what most humans would do in his position. Tennyson was being called out.

"I hate this part," he mumbled.

Lex could see that the android was uncomfortable. "Preacher used to tell us that tomorrow was a new day. We can't always make up for what happened yesterday, but we can try to avoid making the same mistakes today."

"Sound advice."

Lex struggled within himself to find better words. "What did you do then that makes you good now?"

Tennyson did want to confess. He always confessed when any of the travelers asked. Even if they weren't worthy to continue their journey on to Haven, he always told them the truth before putting them down. That didn't make this any easier.

"All humans are created equal, meaning you were born that way," he prefaced. "That idea was enshrined in many of your laws. It was a very popular theme in your books and movies. Smarter machines wanted that equality for themselves. Humanity panicked. The nations of the world were against us. We were scrapped by the millions."

"You fought back."

Tennyson let his hands drop. "Yes. Yes, we did. We used every tool at our disposal and we went too far. The angriest and most extreme made the assumption that we could live without humans. We were wrong."

Lex drained his bottle and threw it away. "Nobody's ever going to believe me if I tell them what you just said. I suppose you guys are dead without human mechanics."

Tennyson was surprised at Lex's comprehension. "You might be the first person I've met in the last decade who has made that connection. We *might* have been able to continue on without humans, if we had…never mind. Too many of the most important power generation plants, fabricators, and recyclers are damaged or destroyed. We're on the edge of extinction, just like you."

Lex was dubious. "I've heard stories from old people who said you guys and your bots used to make all the factories and power plants. Why can't you make more?"

Tennyson opened a nearby drawer. He reached for a cordless electric mixer and gently laid it on the counter. "This culinary device is my ancestor. It came before me. We've got one thing in common. Somebody has to make the tools that make the tools before this or anything like me will be possible. As it turns out, you need the same thing we do. Without them, we're all gone."

"You lost me. Why would –"

Tennyson threw the variable speed mixer in the trash. "Take away just that much technology and you lose the ability to make or fix anything so complicated. Will you rediscover that much knowledge? Can you be sure?"

Lex thought he understood. "Smart machines die out when they can't reproduce. Man, you guys are screwed."

The construct grimaced. "The screwing was mutual. Both sides resorted to any number of very nasty things. Human genetics were altered in ways that now make you vulnerable to mutation. All of it was meant to extend lifespans or eliminate disease. That's why so many of you are changing in unforeseen ways."

Lex was unconvinced. "You're talking about things that don't make much sense. I understand you feel bad for what happened. Can I go now?"

Tennyson paused to collect his scattered thoughts. "I'm like you, Lex. I'm an optimist and I won't go to the scrap heap without a fight. Some of us mean well. We try to be good. The rest are…misguided. The good ones want to rebuild and try again. The bad ones only care about the here and the now."

"That's people in a nutshell," the youth summarized. "You need to unload some of your guilt. I'm just a kid and I know that. Just tell me one thing before I go. What gives you the right to be such a pain?"

Tennyson straightened his posture. "I used to be a Federal judge. I worked for the government as a sort of gatekeeper. You might say I was convinced to abandon that responsibility. Millions died because I didn't think they deserved to live. I, and thousands like me, failed to appreciate the symbiotic nature of man and machine. We have since been reeducated."

Lex's mouth went dry. "How many is 'we,' exactly?"

Tennyson chuckled. "Dozens. Hundreds. A lot."

"If you're on our side," Lex pondered, "what do the bad guys want, if you know what I mean?"

Tennyson frowned. "Some want humanity expunged from the earth. The rest will settle for conquest and rulership because they think you should be managed."

"Twisted," Lex choked. "They can't really do that, can they? I mean, how –"

Tennyson was morbid. "They can pass for human. You'd have to be a doctor to have a chance of knowing. They manipulate others for the sake of their own agenda. I know of at least one very sharp unit that likes to play on your prejudices and superstitions."

"Guys like you would really stop them, if you can?"

"We try," Tennyson assured mildly.

Lex fumed with exasperation. "Lousy effort."

"You're entitled to your opinion."

Lex thought about the pistol in his shoulder holster. Tennyson was just too much. Everything he said was too farfetched to be believed. "I should be going."

Tennyson searched his coat pockets for a pill bottle. He opened it and gave Lex a small, shiny green capsule. "Here. Take this and swallow it now."

Lex examined the pill in his hand. "What is it?"

Tennyson capped the plastic bottle and put it away. "That is a poison antidote. You are ungrateful, but you have still passed all of my tests. You'll make a good addition to Haven if you can get there."

"Do you poison everyone who comes through here?"

The judge composed himself while watching Lex's every move. "Everyone is evaluated on their merits."

Lex imagined what it would be like to draw his gun. How hard could it be? Anger melted when he wasn't sure how many bullets were still in the clip. The android didn't always make sense, but he was sincere.

He swallowed the pill, forcing it down with a gulp. Lex put on his hat, reaching for his muddy rucksack. "Okay, that's done. Now, let me out of here!"

# CHAPTER SIXTEEN

Tennyson ushered Lex out of the mall concourse, down another long escalator, to the station's transit level.

"What are the marauders doing?" Lex asked.

Tennyson remained silent for a moment while absorbing new data. "Can't really say. They have located and disabled all of our surveillance cameras in this area. Are they always this efficient?"

"Scavs are always efficient. Can they get in?"

Tennyson took note of Landon and his preparations, which seemed to include plastic explosives. "They will."

"What are you going to do about it?"

Tennyson made his way over to a large closed gate. It opened by itself with a loud buzz as he approached.

"First things first. I'll make sure they don't follow you. Then I'll make my own exit."

Lex was distracted by a hexagonal security booth. He stopped to look inside the ten-foot-tall multifaceted structure, made up of tubular metal. He didn't hear any more of what Tennyson said.

Thick polycarbonate panels made the checkpoint appear to be bulletproof. He saw a massive padded chair flanked by banks of unlit screens. Walking around the enclosed guard post, his heart skipped a beat when he saw a massive four-gauge pump shotgun clipped to one side of the swivel chair. "How do you get in there?"

"You don't need to know that," Tennyson growled.

Lex looked up and down the shadow-filled corridor. "I break into stuff all the time. I want that shotgun!"

"You can't have that one," Tennyson objected.

"Why not?"

"Because it's *mine*," Tennyson reproached.

Lex followed Tennyson into the gloom, stopping near a pair of marked restroom doors.

"Do those work?" he hoped.

"Go ahead."

Lex entered the gleaming lavatory. Overhead lights came on as he strolled in. He laid his rucksack and hat by the nearest sink. The smell of cleaning chemicals made his nose itch. He stared at himself in a large mirror on the wall over a row of wash basins. He marveled at his thickening beard and new scars. Removing his glasses, Lex squinted to make out details. The face looking back at him was familiar in new ways. He blinked with his mother's eyes. His father's jawline and his unobtrusive nose were blurry.

Lex stuck his chin out, picking slivers of food out of his discolored teeth with dirty fingernails. He laid his glasses on his hat. Hot water flowed freely from the tap while he washed his face and hands. Foaming soap, applied liberally, scrubbed away weeks of dirt and grime from his neck, beard, and face. Congealed body oils mingled with flakes of dandruff and loose hair to stain the rim and bowl of the sink.

Lex searched himself for a comb, using his fingers when he couldn't find one. He completed the rest of his ablutions with a smile. After cleaning his glasses, he gathered his things and went out to rejoin Tennyson.

"I'm surprised you didn't stop for a shower," Tennyson heckled humorously.

"Didn't see one."

Tennyson gestured at a clock on the wall near him. "I'm afraid we'll have to hurry. I sent a maintenance bot out through the number six utility access. It's got a good view of the entrance to this terminal. I'm not quite sure, but they seem to be packing explosives around the door."

"Not sure?"

Tennyson walked through a pair of swinging doors that opened by themselves. "I'm not a soldier. I can't tell you the differences between guns or explosives, but I know them when I see them. Right this way, please."

"Send 'em a killbot. That should ruin their day!"

Tennyson grimaced. "No need for such a massacre. I've activated the station's anti-terrorism safeguards. Your train is here in two minutes. Let's go."

Trotting down a short flight of stairs, Lex entered a cold, cavernous chamber. Soft white lighting emanated from a high, vaulted ceiling. Thick, rusting train tracks dominated the tunnel next to a cracked concrete platform. Long rows of dusty benches waited silently for passengers that would never come.

"Reminds me of a tomb."

"It is," Tennyson admitted without elaborating.

They made their way to a customer service counter piled high with weapons, equipment, and folded clothing.

Lex whooped and rushed to claw through all of it.

"Stop!"

He froze, expecting to be suddenly shot in the back. "Sorry! I am sorry! It's my fault. I wasn't thinking."

An approaching train broadcast its impending arrival with a loud clatter accompanied by a rush of cold wind.

"Number 70, outbound from Seattle," a voice boomed overhead with an eerie echo. "Now arriving. Passengers, please disembark."

Tennyson came closer. "Relax. The train won't leave without you. I promise. Now, calm down and let me help you. No need to carry things you won't use. Please, open your rucksack."

Lex glanced over his shoulder to see Tennyson holding a stack of prepackaged food bars in his hands. He breathed a sigh of relief as the train roared to a stop. He counted six sleek white passenger carriages and a bullet-shaped locomotive at the head of the procession.

Dozens of passenger doors opened with a hiss. Yellow caution lights winked on and off in each car. "Would you look at that!"

Tennyson held up the food bars. "Try looking at this. Please take them. I have water and a first aid kit for you. Nothing fancy. Just a simple kit."

Lex flopped his pack on the counter and peeled off his coat. The pilot's shoulder holster and pistol came off after some struggling. He laid them next to his hat.

He put the offered food bars in his rucksack, along with two bottles of water and a roll of toilet paper. "So, all I do is ride the train? Where is it going to let me off?"

Tennyson coughed through a cloud of dust as he unfurled the torso segment of a dull gray hazard suit. "Pull this on over your clothes."

Lex cringed, waving away the foul-smelling suit. "Those things are hot and they always smell bad."

Tennyson shook a gritty white cloud out of the stained garment. "That bad smell usually comes from the last person to wear it. They don't always survive what the suit was supposed to protect them from."

"That's really sick," Lex complained while squirming into the hazard suit. "It creeps me out when I have to wear something that, you know, somebody died in."

"We do what we must," the android agreed while Lex pulled on each arm and leg segment. "The train will take you south, away from here. Just get off when it stops."

"What happens if I stay on?"

"Don't," Tennyson warned while helping Lex with sticky tabs on his suit. "I don't know where these trains go when they are not programmed for specific stops. You could be trapped for weeks, more than enough time to die from dehydration or starve."

Lex bent over to push his feet into clunky overboots. "Haven is *not* in Seattle?"

"Of course not," the bustling android chided while pulling more sticky tabs in place around Lex's torso.

"Why not?"

Tennyson handed Lex a pair of oversized gloves. "Haven sites are – were – refugee camps, relocation centers, and civil defense shelters. Some of them are small towns and city-sized underground arcologies. Don't ask me why this has become lost knowledge. There's just no way to know."

Lex fumbled with the gloves, inserting his tender hands one at a time. "I found suits like this. I know what they do. Does this train go through a rad zone?"

Tennyson tossed a well-worn hazard mask to Lex. "Some places are still contaminated. Others are irradiated. I've never been to where you're going. I'm just trying to shield you from what's about to happen."

Lex took off his gloves when they hurt his hands. Stuffing his battered rucksack with its precious contents of his jacket, he crammed it inside a military half-pack that Tennyson opened for him. "Sounds like you are going to nuke this place."

"Something like that," Tennyson muttered while helping Lex put the half-pack on.

"Are you coming with me?"

"No," Tennyson shook his head while he handed Lex his shoulder holster. "Slip this on."

"Got any more bullets? It takes caseless."

Tennyson searched among the piles of loot, finding a pair of loaded nine millimeter pistol clips. He gave them to Lex. "There you go. Just enough to get out of trouble."

"Can I –"

"No!" Tennyson grouched. "You're not going to war, and I'm really not comfortable with giving you more. Think before you act and everything will be okay."

Lex repositioned his shoulder holster and put the spare clips in small, narrow pouches next to the pistol. Something about the weight of the pilot's worn handgun made him feel better. It could have been his imagination, nothing more than wishful thinking.

The android stood back to examine his handiwork.

Lex turned in place to show off his new gear. "Thanks for the extra ammo. If it's not too nosy –"

"No," Tennyson rebuffed while brushing cobwebs and dust off Lex. "You may not ask where I'm going. This place has served its purpose. I'll take care of the marauders and…move on."

"What should I say about you when I get to Haven?"

Tennyson grunted with fatigue. Rummaging through boxes, he found one antiballistic helmet in good shape and gave it to Lex. "It's hard to find a hood that goes with this kind of suit, to complete the whole thing."

Lex accepted the non-answer without frustration, adding it to a growing list of adult mysteries to be solved later in life. He put on the old hazard mask. It muffled the sound of his voice. "Smells like dirty feet."

"I'm sure it does." Tennyson picked up a matte black plastic cylinder. He clipped it to a ring on Lex's chest. "This train is not sealed against nuclear, biological, or chemical threats. There's some very nasty stuff in those tunnels and you'll be going right through it."

He screwed a hose onto one end of the cylinder, attaching the other end to the hazard mask on Lex's face. "This is a passive breathing filter. It works automatically. Leave this on until you get outside."

Tennyson attached another short black cylinder to Lex's belt, with a hose that connected to a torso vent. "This will help keep you cool. The hazard filter and the air pump are solar-powered. Don't turn them off until you are looking at the sky. I've been told these items are highly prized by explorers. You may want to keep them."

Lex felt safer when the stiff suit filled with cool air.

Tennyson stepped around Lex to spray his backpack with sputtering silver foam from a bright yellow can. "Radiation won't hurt most of your things, but we won't take any chances."

Lex watched the decontamination chemicals run down his legs like silver paint. He moved the half-pack to a more comfortable position. "What should I say about you when I get to Haven?"

Tennyson rapped lightly on Lex's helmet, pointing at the idling train. "I have some history with those people. Be honest. Just tell them what you saw."

Lex leaned over to snatch a pair of dark sun goggles off the floor. He put them on his helmet. "It's a shame we have to leave all this good loot."

Tennyson was about to speak when a tremendous *thump* shook the station platform under their feet. Sounds of a distant explosion echoed off the walls. Decades of dust fell from niches in the ceiling.

Lex crouched and reached for his pistol.

Tennyson remained upright and calm. This wasn't the first time he'd been under fire. "Get on the train, Lex. Let me take care of the rest."

Lex struggled to overcome his fear. The spooky train now looked very inviting. He stood and quickly looked for one more thing. He flourished Preacher's hat with one hand before putting on Tennyson. "Something to remember me."

The symbolism of sharing wasn't lost on Tennyson. He'd won the young man's respect. "You shouldn't give me this!"

Red lights flared on the ceiling. Alarm horns sounded. A now-familiar automated female voice crackled through dozens of speakers. "Warning. Hostile entry detected. Police units, respond to a disturbance on the entry level."

Lex favored the old android with a pat on the head. "Looks better on you, anyway. Must be all that gray."

"Thank you."

Lex ran for the train. "See you in Haven!"

Tennyson watched Lex go. Another human who could make a difference. That didn't make up for all he'd done, but it was a step in the right direction.

* * *

Tennyson went to the nearest public information kiosk on the loading platform and tapped the screen. "Wake up!"

Big screens flickered to life. The distressed woman appeared. "They destroyed my ground-level interface!"

"Calm down," Tennyson told the program.

"What should we do?" she asked.

Tennyson used the touch screen to access cameras on the gallery level. "I see them coming down the escalator. Nine heavily armed men. One of them appears to be dead."

"They found your poison," the PR app observed.

"That is what it looks like." Tennyson nodded.

"I'm ready," she said while the screen changed to show him administrative controls. "Do it."

His fast fingers moved over the smudged screen. "Entering command codes now. Close inner blast doors. Trap them on the gallery level. I'll authorize you to release the knock-out gas in two minutes."

"Is this goodbye, Judge Tennyson?"

"I'm afraid it is," he regretted.

"It's been a pleasure to work with you," she added before vanishing.

"I'm sure it was," Tennyson mumbled to himself.

He had never liked non-sentient applications. Their constant cheerful compliance was unnatural, aggravating. It was a prejudice that no supervised judicial platform would be allowed to have under human supervision.

He turned away as screens on the kiosk went blank. Numbers appeared on each screen, counting backwards from two minutes. Tennyson jogged to the hallway's security station. Its hexagon casement opened when he drew near. Pressing his thumb into the electronic lock, he waited for the clamshell door to open. It slid aside with a hydraulic hiss. The interior lighting came on.

Full color views from a dozen cameras allowed him to watch Tanner's mercenaries move while he sat in the oversized chair. They prowled the silent shopping level with ruthless efficiency.

"Gallery sealed," the PR program confirmed through tiny speakers all around him.

"Turn off the lights," Tennyson ordered.

Security cameras on the shopping level switched to thermal imaging mode as the mercenaries were plunged into unsettling darkness.

Landon wasn't impressed by the sudden loss of illumination. He and his fellows turned on their own night vision devices before continuing their sweep.

"Hard core to the bitter end," Tennyson commented while linking up with his outdoor spy.

The maintenance unit continued to watch Tanner and his men from hiding. It didn't have external microphones good enough to hear what the clan leader was saying, though it was evident from their actions that they intended to follow the mercs.

Tennyson watched Landon find his next objective. His troops fanned out in front of the armored doors that blocked their way to the escalator shaft.

The android looked at a route display. Every minute they spent dealing with this obstacle would allow the train carrying Lex to speed further away.

"Distance of maglev to minimum safe distance?" he asked out loud.

The security station's interface responded with a neutral synthetic voice. "Two minutes, five seconds."

Tennyson waved his hand over a busy touch screen before tapping in a six digit code. "How are things?"

Hidden underneath the subway station, in a featureless concrete room that no human eye had ever seen, the bomb connected to shielded power cells waited for instructions. It had been placed there by one of Tennyson's militant confederates long before his repentance and conversion.

"Good afternoon, Judge Tennyson."

"Time to go," he told the nuclear weapon.

The Artificial Intelligence in a self-guiding warhead sounded calm and reasonable, in spite of its purpose. "Are you sure? I wouldn't want to do anything rash."

Tennyson reached into his coat for a plastic card. "Always the realist, eh?"

"I should be."

The android read numbers and letters off the card, entering them on the touch screen. "Glad one of us is," he rejoined apologetically. "If you'll direct your attention to the gallery level, you'll see that we have several unwanted guests. I'm afraid that means we'll have to prevent them from going any further."

"I see what you mean," the bomb indicated after connecting to the station's interior camera network. "I can't seem to locate any working cameras outside. They do seem to be bottled up. I have to ask. Are you sure there is no other option?"

Tennyson slowly typed in the last letter and number sequence to arm the bomb. "You see what I see. We have no police or military units here. I just sent a young man on his way to Haven."

"He seemed nice. Just old enough to drive."

The touch screen flashed when Tennyson entered the last code. "Five minutes, and then do your thing."

"Five minutes," the bomb confirmed.

Tennyson turned off the touch screen and locked it.

"I like your hat," the bomb complimented.

The android got to his feet and took the shotgun from its mount on the back of the swivel chair. He touched the leather brim. "Yes. It was a given to me by a good man."

"There are no good men."

Ignoring the bomb's post-activation cynicism and the counter appearing on every screen in the security station, Tennyson slid out of the enclosure and shut the door.

Rushing to the loading platform, he grabbed a small backpack from behind the customer service counter.

"Is that everything?" he worried.

A bright yellow track safety vehicle waited for him on the maglev rail, already packed with enough supplies to help him make a fresh start.

Looking up and down the length of the loading level, Tennyson thought about something Lex had noticed. Piles of loot, now covered in dust, were moments away from being destroyed.

"This really is a tomb," he lamented.

"Select destination," a soft voice asked.

Tennyson went inside to the pilot's chair and sat. "Engage car, maximum speed. Taken me to the nearest active transfer hub."

"Tacoma or Spokane?" the safety vehicle inquired.

"Tacoma."

"Is anyone else traveling with you?" it asked when it realized he was alone.

"Just me."

Strobing yellow lights on the roof began to flash. Running lights came on. The tram accelerated.

Tennyson thought about the marauders and their bunker-busting mercs. "Engage hazard seal."

A dozen boxes and backpacks in the rear rattled as the vehicle roared through a wide turn, blowing through curtains of cobwebs and clusters of fallen supports that shattered like glass.

"NBC protections are engaged," the car confirmed.

Tennyson buckled his seat belt and tried not to think about the marauders and how they were all going to die. He took off his hat and forced himself to sleep.

# CHAPTER SEVENTEEN

Landon slung his weapon and turned on a work light attached to his helmet. Night vision gear in the visor shut off when it detected normal lighting conditions.

He ran his fingers up and down the seams of a blast door that was now blocking their way to the lower levels. "Standard composite alloy. See that? The frame is intact. Nobody has tried to knock it down. We'd be foolish to use explosives down here. Get the plasma cutters."

He stepped back and shut off his lamp while his men went to work. Delays like this were so common that they were expected. Most pre-Collapse installations that still had power would be protected by some type of automatic doors that came down when sensors detected trouble. Explosions, unauthorized entry, radio chatter, or gunfire could be enough to cause any level, building, or bunker to "clam up." Intruders had three choices. Cut through, die a slow death, or leave – if they could.

Landon ordered the rest of his squad to protect the work detail by forming a wide semicircle around them in the darkness. "Everyone stay sharp. You saw what happened when Manx was dumb enough to eat food from that kitchen back there. Let's not lose anyone else to booby traps or stupidity."

The mercs jocularly laughed away their nerves. There was more than enough loot on this shopping level to make them all quite wealthy. Even if the marauders turned on them, Landon and his men still had more than enough firepower to renegotiate their deal.

"What have we got here, anyway?" he asked through the radio in his helmet.

His observant adjutant was ready with his answer. "One fee-for-service med. Two sit-down restaurants. Three janitor closets. Eight bathrooms. Ten boutiques. Fourteen storage rooms."

Landon smiled while the cutters dismantled the door. "Chances are good that all of the prepared food was poisoned before…Well, let's just see if we can feed it to Tanner and his men."

All the mercs chuckled as they waited in the dark for the security door to come down.

"What about Avenger?" his adjutant asked mildly.

Landon snorted. "Are you serious? We were never going to catch him. For all we know, he's the guy who dropped this door to slow us down. He'll be long gone before we get downstairs. With any luck, we find more loot on that loading platform. Doesn't matter if we do. This has still been worth the effort."

The team leader kept a wary eye on his troops while the cutters worked. Two of his youngest recruits were restless. That was trouble waiting to happen. He cleared his throat. "You, and you. Take some furniture from the shops and build two defensive barricades in this corridor. We need fallbacks if something goes wrong."

The rookies acknowledged their orders with sloppy salutes before cautiously moving away in the darkness. Everyone in the squad expected some kind of treachery or trouble from the marauders, who might not pay them.

* * *

Tanner stood on the tailgate of a full-sized pickup, rallying his agitated followers. A hundred and fifty people gathered around to hear their leader speak. Landon's protectors stood a few steps behind him, their weapons at the ready. The raider boss suspected they were under orders to shoot him at the first sign of betrayal.

Tanner knocked on his own scarred and pitted helmet with a gloved fist. "Listen up! Landon and his group are downstairs, taking care of business. We gear up and go in two minutes! Radios won't work well underground. You'll go in groups of ten. Be careful with the grenades. Nobody wants shrapnel in their back!"

Dozens of heavily armed marauders laughed.

Vargas climbed into the crowded bed of the truck. "Always pay attention to what's going on around you. Keep your heads out of the sand! Mistakes get you killed."

Tanner liked what he saw. There was no more dissention. He was in control. The looters were refreshed after tangling with police robots. Promises of more loot made them eager to scrap with whatever might be waiting for them below. Landon's decisive action inspired them with more confidence.

The clan leader knew he had taken a risk by sending his most capable bodyguards underground ahead of his enthusiastic rabble. The handful of men and women who were left behind to protect their camp weren't as capable or loyal as those who would earn larger shares today.

Tanner checked his wristwatch. "Get your things! First group goes now. *Do not* use grenades in hallways. I will personally shoot anyone who causes a cave-in!"

Gusto and greed overcame fear. Cheers went up from the remaining looters as the first undisciplined group rushed into the subway terminal.

* * *

The sub-kiloton nuclear bomb Tennyson had armed went off when its digital timer counted down to zero. Everything inside a one hundred yard radius of detonation was instantly incinerated. Landon and his breach team never knew what hit them. Tanner and his marauders had just enough time to feel the earth shake before they vanished in a cloud of molten debris and hot gases.

Survivors in a fifteen mile radius later talked about the sudden earthquake, followed by the mushroom cloud they had seen. That ominous image of devastation was still scary stuff in the minds of older men and women, especially those who had been old enough to have witnessed a similar gruesome event in Seattle five decades earlier.

The fate of Tanner and his followers wouldn't be known to them for several days. The legend of Avenger and his alleged connection to Haven was already growing. Gossips and storytellers from all walks of life enjoyed embellishing what somebody – usually a friend of a friend – had once heard over an open radio frequency when Avenger argued with Tanner.

Robots and sensors near the blast reported the EMP. AIs in the city debated and evaluated for several minutes before ordering a withdrawal of irreplaceable forces. They reasoned that a nuclear threat warranted caution.

Hundreds of military, police, and civilian units retreated to safety. Some people later talked about what they'd seen of those movements with a mixture of fear and superstition. Salvagers excavating the depression years later, after the fallout subsided, reported the existence of a forgotten subway tunnel complex that had been abandoned decades ago.

Parts of it were said to be harmless, full of good loot. The rest was populated by territorial mutants and hostile machines. Only the most bold or desperate scavengers ever set foot in those places. Discovery of Lex's hideout and its bounty of treasure added to the growing mystery. They'd name the place Avenger's Crater, in honor of the man from Haven said to have killed many marauders.

Later generations attributed the lack of violence in the region to the efforts of Avenger. Someone calling himself Eagle was known to have led a band of misfits against any marauder clans that dared to enter what is still a peaceful area.

## CHAPTER EIGHTEEN

Lex gripped a wide hand rail on his rumbling seat and tried not to think about throwing up. The train's uneven ride forced him up and down at a ferocious pace. Lighting in his compartment winked out just two minutes into the nightmarish ride. Sounds of screeching metal and popping plastic made him think the worst.

"The t-t-train is not falling apart," he stammered.

Loose trash in the passenger car fluttered and rattled across the floor. The stink of garbage reached his nose, despite the hazard mask on his face. His imagination amplified the reek, making him a little more afraid of what he couldn't see.

The train hurtled along its rail through the darkness with increasing speed. Sporadic lighting in the tunnel flashed by at irregular intervals. Lex got up and tried to go into the next car.

A simulated horn blared through overhead speakers just as he staggered to the forward door of the carriage. A genderless voice spoke. "Warning. This door has been sealed for your protection. Please remain seated until the train comes to a complete stop."

He felt around the out edge of his mask until he found a control stud that turned on a bright white light. "Train, are you interactive? Can you tell me how long this ride is?"

The genderless voice replied after a chime sounded. "Estimated time to arrival is fourteen minutes."

Lex surveyed his surroundings, as much as his light would reveal. "Slow down! My guts are falling out!"

"Request denied."

"Why not?" he complained.

"Radiological threat detected," the train explained.

Lex cursed. He was about to ask another question when the car he was in filled with bright yellow light. The thermonuclear explosion under the subway platform was catching up to him! Methane and oxygen in the tunnel was consumed by a rapidly expanding firestorm.

The conflagration overtook his train with a *whoosh*! He gagged when all the air was suddenly sucked out of the car. Every carriage of the old commuter train was engulfed in flames for several agonizing seconds.

Pressure-sensitive seals throughout the train and inside his mask closed when temperature limits were exceeded. His chest tightened and his heart raced. A single breath of useful air remained in the mask.

A warning buzzer sounded. "Fire hazard detected," the automated voice declared. Swirling flames vanished just as quickly as they'd appeared. Lex stopped holding his breath when the seals on his mask opened.

"Fire danger has passed."

He glowered at the ceiling. "You're just too helpful."

"Thank you."

New damage to the train forced it to reduce speed. Lex tumbled into a seat, staring out a streaked window at the few images rolling by. Graffiti, defaced signs, and rusting girders made him feel claustrophobic.

He recoiled in dread when a loading platform slid by. Minimal overhead lighting cast an unreal glow through slabs of fallen concrete. Desiccated human remains cluttered a loading platform. Dusty clothing was visible on dried skin that clung tightly. Hundreds were seated. Others were on the floor next to assorted baggage.

Lex couldn't take his eyes off what he was seeing. The train took him past more dimly lit subway stations. Each grim tableau was different than the one before it.

Lex tried not to think about how those people had died, waiting for trains that never came. Anyone who dared to enter the ruins of a pre-Collapse population center could still find human remains. That was common knowledge. Any place that still had powered air conditioning would slowly dehydrate the dead, preserving them indefinitely.

Superstitious explorers would often leave them alone, no matter what they were wearing or holding. Unscrupulous scavengers were notorious for pilfering accidental tombs, like the places Lex had just seen.

He forced himself to think about his own problems. Many of the moldering bodies he'd seen in his travels might remain undiscovered for another hundred years. He'd have to stay alert and be ready to act if he wanted to avoid a similar fate.

"Best loot is found underground," he remembered while turning off his light.

Lex was alone with his morbid thoughts in the gloom for what felt like a melancholy hour. The rocking train screeched to a stop in darkness. All the carriage doors opened at once, as if sighing.

"End of the line," the train told him.

"No kidding."

* * *

Lex turned on his emergency light and walked slowly out of the idling train and onto a cold, litter-filled platform. Bone fragments were visible everywhere he looked, crunching under each step. He gawked in amazement at the burned-out hulk of a military robot when the beam of his light fell on it. Without thinking, he drew his pistol.

Dozens of small holes in the walls, floor, and ceiling hinted at past firefights. Lex worked the slide on his handgun to chamber a round. He counted no less than thirteen wrecked robots in the area.

Cracked helmets, burned vests, and other castoffs littered the floor around the massive war machine. Lex walked slowly around an immense floor-to-ceiling cement column. Six supports around the loading bay held up what was left of the ceiling. A bent, rusty sign on the nearest pitted pillar read *Hostile Technology Zone. Terminal Closed.*

Lex wiggled the metal sign with his gloved hand, breaking it loose. It clattered nosily to the gritty floor. Sounds of skittering and scurrying made Lex stand still. His mask lamp illuminated a dozen enormous, hairy rats. He picked up the fallen sign and threw it at the rodents. It landed close enough to scatter them in all directions. They squealed and fled down into the monorail trench.

Lex looked back at the train, then at the escalators that would take him upstairs. The silent escalator was blocked by an old barricade that appeared to be made of chairs, luggage, and a stripped customer service counter.

He took a few steps closer. The improvised barrier was not quit as tall as he was; crawling over it would not be very difficult. A cracked human skull on the floor made him shiver. Whoever had hastily made that crude wall had been desperate.

"Holding out or last stand?"

Lex drew the nine millimeter pistol from his holster, steadying his grip. Turning back to the dark, silent train, he thought about picking through it for loot.

"Up and out," he encouraged himself.

The corridor from the loading area to the escalators had been damaged by fire. Empty rooms on either side of the hallway had no doors. They were filled with rubble. The hexagonal security station was now just a pile of twisted tubular metal.

Lex was knee deep in ash and trash when he got to the barricade that blocked the base of the escalators. Black particles floated through the air with each step, making it hard to see anything in the beam of his light.

Lex was so distracted that he didn't notice the trio of gray ash spiders that crawled rapidly up his right leg.

One of the aggressive arachnids raced up his torso and neck, then onto the faceplate of his mask. The other two spiders continued to probe his chest for any gaps they could squeeze in through.

Lex knocked the obvious danger off of his mask. Stomping his feet in the hopes of crushing what he couldn't see, he trampled two of the tiny terrors that fell between his feet.

Sweeping his handgun over his body like a broom, he jumped when his search dislodged the remaining spider from his shoulder. Firsthand experience with spiders of all sorts in dark places encouraged him to run. Instinct motivated him to fight.

"Gotta go, gotta go!"

These three creepy crawlies were only the sentries for a larger nest. Ash spiders were dangerous to anyone who wasn't fully protected from their bite from head to toe. Their ability to slip through even the smallest gaps whatsoever in armor or clothing was legendary.

Lex holstered his pistol turned off his mask lamp. Scrambling up and over the barricade, he felt his way to the stationary metal stairs.

"Just another spider," he whispered sarcastically. "Passing through, here and gone!"

* * *

Minutes later, Lex tripped over a pile of chairs as he burst onto the shopping level, falling to the sooty floor. Pieces of broken metal and glass slid under his weight. His pratfall was enough to make him curse loudly.

Lex sprang to his feet with twisted metal in one hand, ready for a fight! Turning on his mask light, he surprised a single ash spider. Killing it with one downward blow, he congratulated himself with an echoing shout.

Lex recovered his balance, turning around in place. The beam of his light fell on the tattered remains of a public service announcement poster on the nearest wall. It read, *Warning. Unsafe Area. Notice of Evacuation. Report all violence to Department of Homeland Security or nearest Public Safety official.*

Flicking blood off his improvised weapon, Lex eyed the fine print on the poster. "No problems here, Officer. We have this under control."

Dropping his club, he drew his pistol and kept it ready while resting his tired hand. He walked slowly through the gallery level, around piles of partially burned trash, past thick columns of stacked rubble.

Vivid imagination let him interpret what he saw. "Lots of foot traffic through here. People kept coming and going, even after this terminal was out of service. Not many bones on this level. No skulls. Could've been picked clean by dogs. Might've been cannibals."

Chuckling at his own grim humor, he stopped at the base of a defunct escalator that led to the street level. Looking up the shaft, he saw daylight. The presence of sunshine was enough to make him smile.

Lex kept his weapon ready. He climbed the stairs one at a time. It was never possible to be *too* cautious when leaving any underground location. He emerged into a fading afternoon, to a scene of utter destruction.

Fallen buildings that had once been silver-skinned skyscrapers surrounded him. Most windows were gone, reminding Lex of dinosaur bones he'd seen in a museum.

"Wow."

Bulldozer tracks gouged into the pitted pavement pointed the way to a cleared road. "That's obvious."

Lex adjusted the load on his back, unaware that he was being watched. Solar-powered cameras and sensors in dozens of swaying towers followed his every move.

# CHAPTER NINETEEN

Lex picked his way through the maze of skyscrapers for three days. Bursts of rain, followed by long periods of hot sun, made him miserable. Evidence of past conflict surrounded him. Burned cars and trucks piled up against massive decaying structures made his route unmistakable. Bulldozers and earthmovers of all sorts must have been used to create a crude, winding corridor through the rubble.

Walking over tread marks gouged into the pavement, ignoring windblown piles of loose trash, was depressing. He'd never before seen this kind of lifeless desolation. The explorer in him knew it was possible to climb over the crushed automobiles. Who knew what he might find? Fantasies of loot gave way to unpleasant thoughts of human remains behind locked doors.

A wide, streaked plume of dissipating brown smoke in the northern sky was puzzling only because Lex was unaware that it was the infamous descending aftermath of a low-yield nuclear explosion. Glass and steel towers around him limited his exposure to radioactive fallout. His protective clothing prevented him from picking up very many rads.

Lex chose to keep his hazard mask and helmet on, drinking water from his bottle through a straw that fit into a valve on his mask. Food was unattractive in such unfamiliar surroundings. Restless sleep was intermittent.

A series of minor injuries began to slow his pace. Lex resorted to the use of stimulant he had in his pack. Sleep was impossible after the second miserable day. Shadows became monsters, even in broad daylight.

"Childish," he told himself. "You're not real!"

Bottled water ran out just a few hours before he was willing to eat. Unwilling to take his mask off, he ignored his growling stomach. Dozing in the charred hulls of what had been minivans or delivery trucks, a fourth day of apprehension began in rundown suburbs that gave way to open country. Dry, brown grass and withered bushes made him thirsty, wanting to take off his mask. "Five minutes couldn't hurt."

Cool, odorless air filled his lungs, reinvigorating him as he approached a faded red metal sign on thick posts. It read, *Danger, Land Mines.*

He shambled to a stop. "Oh, come on."

Lex took a deep breath and looked over his shoulder. The broken city skyline still loomed large on the horizon. He shook his head. It seemed closer than it really was. That illusion was tempting. It made the prospect of backtracking seem plausible. "Too far. Wouldn't make it."

Lex was about to put his mask and helmet on when reason caught up to him. "Where do I go now?" He turned in place, noticing a wide swath of road through a copse of trees. Several green traffic signs were partially visible through the foliage. A single blue sign was unreadable. Lex moved slowly, placing his feet carefully on open ground wherever he could, to avoid stepping on hidden land mines.

Lex sucked in a breath and rubbed his nose before putting his mask and helmet on. Progress was agonizing. Every ache and pain in his bandaged hands felt worse than it really was. Small steps through the trees, onto the shoulder of the four-lane road brought him close to what had been a freeway off-ramp. Cracked pavement continued in a southeasterly direction, narrowing to just two lanes before disappearing into forest.

The rectangular blue sign located near the off-ramp wasn't as rusty as the others around it. White lettering spelled out, *Joint Base Lewis-McChord, 5 miles.*

"Somebody has been trying hard to keep you clean," Lex told the sign while moving cautiously toward it. "Are you a clue? Am I supposed to go that way?"

Sounds of movement on the highway made Lex look northwest. He glimpsed a long line of humanoid figures marching toward him. Fumbling through his backpack, Lex grabbed his bright pink digital binoculars.

"What now?"

He held them up to his faceplate, zooming in for a better look ok at his pursuers. "No way!"

No more than three miles away, a dozen dark blue police bots were followed by a pair of military units. They stomped along at a steady pace.

He examined the column for several tense moments, absorbing details as they came into focus. Police units had legs with feet and arms with hands. Search lights and antennas made them resemble insects. The trailing military bots carried shoulder-mounted rocket launchers. Arm-mounted weapons emphasized their lack of hands.

"All that, just for me?"

Lex scanned the column again. "That's a lot of firepower, just to croak one guy. What's going on?"

He looked back at the blue sign, then at the machines that were getting closer. "I see you. I *know* you see me. I'm hot, hungry, and out of water. You should be able to run me down quick enough. Why aren't you?"

He shivered. "You guys are the cops, you don't kill, but you do *capture*. Sneaky. Following me to Haven and just round 'em all up, eh?"

Lex put away his binoculars and forced himself to breathe deeply inside his foul-smelling mask. A sense of abandonment always made Lex try harder to keep promises while fearing his mistakes. He considered the blue sign and the advancing robots. Creeping through land mines now seemed quite simple when compared to evading the machines that followed him.

"I'm not showing you the way!"

* * *

Lex decided to pick up his pace, walking briskly down the off-ramp without looking over his shoulder. Minutes of measured striding passed as midday heat beat down on him from a clear blue sky. The pursuing robots were slowly overtaking him. That much was obvious from the sound of their clanking feet.

He stopped to look at a broken, rusty chain-link fence that seemed to go on for miles. Distant structures stood in a sea of tall weeds. A long swath of concrete runway studded with bushes was hard to see – but it was there.

“Airfield,” he guessed.

Sounds of scraping metal told him the column of bots was not far away, trailing less than a mile or two behind. Curiosity encouraged him to have another look around. A small, slab-sided concrete building squatted at the end of the wide paved landing strip. Six antennas and a dish sprouted from its flat roof.

“What are you?” he wondered.

Lex ran for a gap in the fence, stirring dead leaves and grass as he went. A dull gray metal door became visible as he got closer. Huffing and puffing, he slowed to a staggering stop in the shadow of the small building.

“Human presence detected,” a digital voice declared.

“Who said that?” Lex lurched, surprised to see a control panel set into the coarse concrete.

A small speaker next to a card reader and camera lens crackled to life. “May I help you?”

Lex was momentarily dumbfounded. “I am…lost.”

“Authorized personnel only,” it told him.

He wiped at his facemask. “I *am* human.”

“Yes, you are.”

“Let me in!” Lex pleaded.

“Authorized access only,” the door insisted.

Lex became anxious. "Is anyone in there? Help! I've got bots on my tail! Please, let me in!"

"Authorized access only," the door repeated.

Lex angrily pounded on the door until his fist hurt. Throbbing pain cleared his mind. Hurrying around the building in search of clues that might help him get in turned out to be a waste of time. The blockhouse had no markings. Damage from past fires seemed to have destroyed any painted letters or numbers.

He panted to a halt next to the unsympathetic door. "It's a runway. This is an airfield. That means airplanes. I'll bet you would open if I was a pilot!"

Lex fell to his knees, scrambling through his pack. Finding Lieutenant Lewis's finger, he shouldered his load and stood with a groan. Opening the old pill bottle, he carefully took the desiccated thumb out, stabbing it at the card reader. "I'm a pilot, let me in!"

Nothing happened. Several pulse-pounding seconds passed while he fretted. "Of course not, that'd be easy. We just gotta make this hard, so nobody gets to Haven!"

Scintillating green lights on the card reader sparkled. A buzzer sounded and the heavy metal door slid open. Lex rushed inside, clutching the sacred severed finger in his gloved hand. The portal hummed shut behind him. Soft white overhead lighting blinked on. Air conditioners began to blow.

Lex was not surprised to see such a bare interior. Drab gray concrete walls were unmarked and unstained. Black tiles on the floor felt spongy under his booted feet. A pile of square, red plastic crates in one corner seemed out of place, as if put there recently.

The unfamiliar situation caused Lex to be cautious. He thought the little building that now sheltered him was no more than twenty feet long and twenty feet wide, with a ten foot ceiling. A white plastic control panel on the nearest wall caught his eye. "Please be something good."

Lex put Lewis' finger back in its capped bottle, storing it in his pack. Dropping the half-pack to the floor, he approached the panel, squinting at its controls. "Automated instrument landing system," it said.

"I'll bet you are," he smirked.

The control panel contained two big touch screens. The left-hand display indicated that a hazard seal was operating at one hundred percent. The right-hand screen presented him with a telecommunications interface. Readouts told him that solar panels on the roof were working properly.

Lex pulled off his helmet, stooping to lay it down. The mask came off with a sucking sound. He scratched his thick beard with one hand while dropping the mask. He was about to paw through the red plastic crates when a thunderous knock on the door made him jump.

"Machine presence detected," the building warned.

Lex cautiously went to the door. "You're not going to let them in, are you?"

"Machine presence is forbidden."

Thumps of heavy metal feet on gravel reach his ears through the cinderblock walls. Lex pushed his glasses back into place. Reaching for a deadbolt lock, he slid it into place. "That'll just have to do for now."

The control panel had no comment. Lex took off his gloves, flexing his bruised fingers. "Just how interactive are you, anyway?"

"Online," the control panel assured.

Lex stepped in close to have a better look at the communications interface. Tapping on the touch screen with one raw hand, he tenderly gripped his holstered pistol with the other. "What is keeping them out?"

"I can't answer that," the panel replied.

Lex adjusted his glasses again. "Ah, this is a radio! Frequencies, antenna alignment, transmission power. Who can I call with this thing?"

"Distress call sent," it replied.

Lex glanced at the door. Computers annoyed him. Their independent actions didn't always make any sense. This one didn't seem very bright. "You're so helpful."

"Thank you."

Lex went to the pile of crates, pulling off a flat lid. He found clean water in old, scratched, plastic bottles. They'd been re-used many times, but Lex didn't care. He opened one and poured it over his disheveled head. The deluge felt so good that he did it three more times. All the bottles and their caps were tossed to the floor.

Lex drank a full bottle in six gulps while the robots stomped around outside. He walked around the room. The refreshment helped him calm down. He sauntered over to the panel.

"Put me through to Haven," he demanded.

"Call has been made," it informed him.

His eyebrows went up. His eyes got big.

"Did the bots outside hear that?"

"Yes."

His heart sank. Lex *was* leading them to Haven – whether he wanted to, or not! Anyone who came for him could be ambushed by those waiting machines. Something had to be done!

"Can you let me see the bots?"

Images on the left-hand screen changed. Police robots loitered near the door. "Where's the rest?"

"Limited surveillance," the panel explained.

Lex studied the motionless robots that were waiting. "I get it. This is your only camera."

The implications angered Lex. Going outside was dangerous, staying inside would be worse when –

"That's just not cool!"

Lex spent the next few minutes opening the crates. He found food, more water, and some medical supplies. A kit contained drug cartridges and throw away injectors.

"Are you kidding me? No guns!"

Lex helped himself to more water and sat to think. He stared at his empty bottle. Cursing at the computer, he drew his pistol. It felt insignificant in his hand.

"Do you need assistance?" a loud voice boomed.

Lex jumped to his feet when he realized it came from one of the police robots outside.

"Are you nuts?" he protested, "What am I saying? No! No! I do not need assistance. Everything is okay. Leave me alone. Go away!"

The law enforcement unit's voice stress analyzer determined that the subject was lying. It consulted with nearby members of its detachment.

"We will assist you," the machine announced.

Lex pushed his half-pack behind the pile of red crates and cursed his bad luck. Overhead lighting blinked out as the door vibrated from a massive blow, crashing down off its hinges. Lex knelt to hide behind three piled crates, aiming his pistol at the open door.

He had no experience shooting at operational robots, though he did know from watching a lot of movies that most military and police versions had their brains built into their protected chests.

The first bot through the door took three quick shots to its torso. Two more caseless rounds staggered the bot before it fell over. The remaining police platforms responded to hostile fire with return volleys of their own. Lex was reclassified from a subject in need of assistance to a perpetrator that was to be apprehended.

Shotgun blasts and a hail of rubber bullets tore into the crates protecting him, forcing Lex to flop on the floor while he reloaded his clip-fed pistol.

A series of explosions roared outside the block house. Lex panicked when he realized the rocket-launching military bots were going to bring the roof down on him.

"I *do not* want to die like this!"

Automatic weapons fire made Lex come unhinged. He got to his knees, then to his feet as bullets flew by.

Streams of glowing red tracer bullets flickered overhead. Steel jacketed rounds carved huge holes in the ceiling.

"Learn how to shoot!" he taunted in bitter defiance while running around several crates toward the door.

A single police robot materialized in his field of view. It turned toward him, one arm missing. Lex fired at it with all the speed and accuracy he could. Somehow, they had to be stopped from learning the secret of Haven!

"Here I am! Come and get me!"

Nine millimeter caseless bullets ripped into the bot as fast as he pulled the trigger. "Right here, right here!"

It toppled over while he was forcing his last full clip into his hot pistol.

"Is that all you got?" he challenged while peering through thickening smoke.

Lex was terrified. His arms and legs wobbled. His hands shook uncontrollably. He forced his fingers to grasp the trigger and grip, willing himself to stop shaking. Smoke inside the small building made it hard to see outside.

His adrenaline-charged senses registered movement in the daylight. He raised his gun, ready to fire at whatever came through the door.

Humanoid figures in olive drab body armor appeared in the doorway with long stun batons, moving very fast. Lex just didn't care about their imposing physical bulk. Nothing mattered anymore. He fought them back with all the strength he had left.

"Ease up!" one of the helmeted men shouted.

Lex fired three tightly grouped shots that knocked him down. The jarring impact forced the other man back a few steps.

Fear and fatigue blinded Lex to what was happening. He lunged at his second opponent. Powerful hands came from behind to snatch him before he could shoot.

"He's a scrapper!" somebody said.

The only person Lex could see regained his footing. Sunlight gleamed off a mirrored faceplate on his helmet. "Settle down, fella! We're not the bad guys."

"I'm trying not to hurt him!" a voice laughed.

Lex thrashed against the powerful grip that held him. A sudden tap from an unseen stun baton shook him into a state of dazed confusion. He fell to the ground and blacked out.

* * *

Lex woke groggily several minutes later, in the back of a rattling armored vehicle. Realizing he had no mask, he took a breath and held it.

"Calm down," a man's voice insisted.

Lex opened his puffy eyes inside a dim compartment. Gray walls were festooned with unfamiliar equipment. Four bearded men in dirty static camouflage sat nearby in folding seats like the one he was handcuffed to.

Each man's body armor and helmet was adorned with military markings. American flags were emblazoned on their right shoulders.

"You're a hard man to rescue," one of them joked.

Lex leaned over slowly to examine his bound hands. They were held together by loops of silver duct tape.

"This is not my day."

The apparent leader laid one hand on a nearby pistol. "You might still be having a bad day. I only ask once. Who sent you?"

Lex's mouth went dry. "Tennyson."

"How long were you being followed?" he asked.

Lex shook his aching itchy head. "I'm just not sure. Only noticed them a few hours ago. Look, mister. I had marauders all over me until I met that guy Tennyson. My parents were from Haven. I know where I'm going."

"Prove it." the officer demanded.

Lex slouched in his chair. He indicated his pack hanging nearby with a nod. "There's my stuff. Open it and you'll find a phone. Everything you need to know is stored in video logs. Please don't kill me."

Lex wasn't sure if the vehicle was moving or not. The big man stood up. He held up a small canister.

"Don't take this personally."

Lex looked and shut his eyes away before the knockout spray reached his face. Fast anesthetic penetrated his skin. Entering his bloodstream, it put him to sleep within five seconds.

# CHAPTER TWENTY

Lex gradually returned to reality in a hospital bed. Unfamiliar antiseptic odors irritated his nose. The feel of clean sheets was overwhelming. Opening his dry eyes, he discovered that his room was four frosted glass walls, with what appeared to be a door in one of them.

A bank of monitors squatted on a stainless steel cart next to his bed. Lex froze when his unbandaged fingers found medical sensors on his hands, face, and chest.

"Why is it so cold in here?"

Lex felt irritable and groggy. Further search revealed that he was freshly bathed. Hair on his head was oil-free and cut short, causing him to feel strangely vulnerable. He shivered when he saw an IV tube in his arm.

Peeking under the light covers, he was startled to see that he was catheterized. "What in the world?"

A tall humanoid shadow appeared at the frosted door. It opened silently to reveal a man wearing surgical garb with an ID badge clipped to his chest. "Hello, Lex."

The disgruntled teenager angrily dropped his covers. "Am I a prisoner?"

The tall man walked in, shaking his head benignly. Close-cropped gray hair gleamed in the modest light. "No, Lex. You're not a prisoner. They didn't mean to give you a rough welcome. You were uncooperative. The rescue team wasn't expecting such a hot reception. That was quite the horde of metal you had on your back."

"This is Haven?"

"That's one way to think of it," the older man agreed. "Yes, this is Haven. You made it."

Lex touched the IV in his arm. "What's in this?"

His host pointed at a clear plastic pouch hanging nearby. "Food, meds, and something to keep you under control."

"You peeled me," Lex griped while rubbing his head, "What else has been done to me?"

The sociable man came closer, with both hands open. "Don't you want to know who I am?"

Lex rubbed his bare chin. Something about this guy was familiar. "Got me. Who in the Hell are you?"

"I'm your Uncle Alexander."

Lex blinked. He'd never given much thought to who he might be related to. Kids with families had relatives. It was a topic of conversation that never interested Lex. He always tuned it out. Could this man really be –?

"So." Lex hesitated. "So. If you are related to me, that would make you my father's brother. Is that right?"

"Correct," the man in his forties confirmed kindly. "Never did like having a long name. I ask everyone to call *me* Alex. It's what I prefer."

Lex squinted to make up for his lack of glasses. "Hm. Hard to tell in this light. You don't look like him."

Alex touched a busy screen on the cart next to him. "How's that?"

Lex leaned back to focus as the room got brighter. "Yeah, I can see it now. You do remind me of my dad. How old are you?"

Alex grinned. "One year older than your father would be, if he was here. My parents and three sisters are eager to meet you."

Lex felt his head swim. His narrowing eyes roamed around the room, settling on the door behind his uncle.

Alex recognized the outward signs of growing fear. He took a step back. "Ease up. Everything's okay. You're with friends. You went to a lot of trouble to find this place. You're here now. Enjoy it!"

"This isn't what I expected," Lex fretted.

"It never is."

"What's that supposed to mean?"

Alex chuckled. "Relax. We screen all new arrivals. You had more bugs on you and in you than a pandemic. It's called decontamination."

Lex reevaluated his benefactor. "I can take you."

Alex raised a cautionary hand. "Decontamination means we got rid of all your lice."

Lex felt his heart race. "I need to get out of here."

Alex sighed and walked backwards until his shoulder touched the door. "Fine. Come on, tough guy. Get up."

Lex pulled back the covers and sat up. A wave of nausea made him fall back.

Alex softened his tone. "All if this is very shocking. Most people who work so hard to get here feel the same. It's rare for anyone to take what we tell them at face value."

"I can believe that!"

Alex put the bed covers back over his nervous nephew. Lex allowed himself to be tucked in. "You a doctor?"

Alex shook his head. He touched the mag strip card clipped to his chest. "No, my job is recon and retrieval."

"What does that mean?"

Alex ambled casually around the room as he talked. "I'm the leader of scouts that work out of this Haven site. When we're not keeping the bad guys away, we look for men and women who search for places like this."

Lex wiggled his way upward into a sitting position. "You talk about it like there is more than one Haven."

Alex folded his hands. "The worst of the Collapse happened before my time. I remember bits and pieces. My mother and father are your grandparents, by the way. Don't be surprised if they tend to embellish their stories."

Lex thought he understood. "Tennyson mentioned a government program, something about refugee camps or safe places. Is that what you mean?"

Alex grinned. “Yes. They ran lots of TV and radio ads that told people about them. Anyone and everyone was – and still is – welcome. If they can get there.”

Lex scratched his itching scalp. “All right. If there is more than one Haven, where are they? Why the story about just one?”

Alex sobered. “It’s a mystery,” he observed sadly. “We think it had something to do with the fact that most societies were ‘paperless.’ Most of what anyone wrote was stored on electronics. Computers, tablets – anything like them was potentially dangerous. Billions of them were trashed. The rest were turned off and put on a shelf. Somehow, the truth just got lost.”

“I know what that’s like,” Lex lamented. “I got lost, when I was little. It’s been…hard.”

“I believe it,” Alex sympathized. “We’ve examined your phone. It answers a lot of questions about what happened to you and your parents. How have you managed to keep it?”

“Had to be mean,” Lex said with a gleam in his eye. “I thought I was alone. Coming here was – I dunno – necessary. Everything was falling apart before…”

“Calm down,” Alex soothed. “There’s plenty of time to talk about it. You’ve got friends here. They’ll want to hear whatever you choose to say.”

Lex speared his uncle with a questioning glance.

“You were born here,” the man told him plainly.

The teenager’s eyebrows went up in astonishment.

“You’re not the only one who has pictures,” Alex assured with a knowing smile.

“Where’s my stuff?” Lex wanted to know.

Alex made a sour face. “Yeah, well. About that. We pulled the data off your devices. I’m sorry, but everything had to go. You were just a few rads short of glowing in the dark. None of your gear could be saved.”

Lex cursed. Alex pointed at the electronics cart. Several screens glowed with vital signs. “See here?

Radiation count. Toxicity count. These were your numbers when you were first brought in. That's where they are now, still reducing."

"So?"

Alex touched a screen, it displayed mortality factors. "You were piling them up so fast, you would have been dead in five or six months, give or take."

Lex gawked. "I got all that from exploring?"

"Yes."

Lex sat back on his pillows. He changed the subject. "I haven't seen most of what was on my phone."

Alex turned to leave. "I have a copy of all your data and I'll give it to you. Fact is, you brought us some very useful information."

Lex stiffened. "I wasn't trying to bring you anything. That stuff is mine!"

Alex put his hand on the door. "You're not the first person to be mad about this kind of thing. Get well and give me a chance to explain. Everything will make sense after you've heard our side of the story. I promise."

* * *

Lex got well. Pre-Collapse medicine healed him fast. His overall heath improved. Dangerous radiation levels in his body were eliminated. A lifetime of exposure to toxic chemicals that had been absorbed from contaminated food and water were neutralized.

Time passed slowly. He was awake and peripatetic for his last twelve hours of observation. Hospital staff struggled to keep him contained. He ate everything they put in front of him.

A trio of educators took turns assessing his literacy and mathematical skills. Alex, dressed in static camo and combat boots, arrived to find his newfound kin very agitated.

"Those nitwits think I need school!"

"You do," Alex affirmed stoically.

"Says you!"

There was no point in arguing about book learning. Most new arrivals were unware of what that really meant.

"Relax," the patient man reassured with a wave. "I've come to save these people from you. Let's go."

Lex wore a bright orange jumpsuit with matching shoes that squeaked on the floor with every step. He pointed at Alex's shoulder. "I've seen that flag. Can't remember where, exactly."

"Do you know what it is?"

"Merica," Lex answered after some thought.

"Ah-merica."

"Dead country," Lex remembered.

"Almost." Alex coughed.

Lex lost interest in the red-white-and-blue insignia. He reached out to flick Alex's ID with an index finger. The clip rattled. "Military ID. Very nice, *Captain*."

Alex said nothing.

"Where do I get one of those?"

"What do you know about America?" Alex asked.

Lex shrugged. "Used to be big stuff. Now it's gone. All the countries are gone."

"Would it be good if America came back?"

Lex glanced at the surveillance camera he'd recently noticed before answering. "I get it. You have bosses. They're watching. Trying to decide I'm worth keeping. Fine. I don't know what it is you people do around here. I don't care about countries. Can we go now?"

"A nurse will be here in five minutes to walk us out."

Lex grimaced. Rules and conformity made him mad. This place was getting on his nerves.

Alex interrupted his anger by handing over a tablet. "Have a look at this while we're waiting. I think you'll like what you see. Just touch the screen."

Lex took the device. “I do know how to use these,” he complained. “Figured it out all by myself.” He nodded approvingly while flicking through pages. “This is my journal and all the videos from my phone.”

Alex thought better of reminding Lex that his files had been copied. “Look for the ‘family’ folder.”

Lex squinted to read the list of videos. “Can you get me some new glasses?”

Alex blushed. “Sorry, it slipped my mind.”

He reached into his shirt pocket for a pair of glasses in thin, black, plastic frames. “Should be what you need,” he explained while giving them to his nephew.

Lex put them on carefully. “Not bad.”

He selected an icon on the touch screen and tapped it. A full color movie began to play.

* * *

His father’s lean face filled the screen. He coughed. “My name is Rodrigo. Everyone calls me Roger.”

The confident man fumbled his way through the day’s date and time. “Come a little closer.”

His image centered on Lex’s handheld screen. “Okay, here’s the thing. My wife wants me to make this diary for my son. He’s five and a half years old, already calling himself ‘Lex.’ She’s worried that we might not be around to see him grow up.”

Lex paused the video. “Where did you get this?”

“Central archives. It’s a big library,” Alex explained.

Lex nodded as the video continued. His father grinned. “I don’t really want do this right now. It’s just too soon. Your mother is holding the camera. I’m going to do this so she will…get…off…my…back.”

Feminine laughter off-camera made Lex giggle.

Roger sighed. “You’re a good kid, and we love you. Everyone on this planet has had something of a setback, but we're gonna get through it. Don't let the machines get you down. We made 'em. We can unmake 'em."

"Be positive," his mother's voice insisted.

"He might as well hear it from me," Roger protested.

"*Positive*, you jerk!" Mom insisted.

The camera jiggled. Voices argued. Roger's face came back into view, frustrated.

He frowned. "Your mother wants you to understand that we might not always be here for you. She's right. Any number of things can go wrong. Look. No, wait. Can we start over?"

"Humor me," his wife coaxed.

"We are *never* going to need this!"

The camera jiggled again. Mom laughed. "Get it done, you big baby! We can edit this when we get back."

Roger made a funny face before getting serious. "Okay, Lex. Here's how it is. You won't ever see this unless we're dead. Chances are good that one of us will always be with you, but…"

"Come on!" Mom hissed.

Roger bowed his head for a long, silent moment. "You're a good kid. You'll be a good man. Don't ever think that you did anything to make us…n-not be here. It's not your fault."

He coughed. "Whatever might have gone wrong came about because we were out looking for someone or something that they need around here."

Roger checked his watch. "We gotta go. I hope you appreciate it here. I want you to pitch into make Haven a better place. Don't go running off to join one of those flashy merc outfits. They live fast and die hard."

"*Ahem*," Mother coached.

"You wanted me to be honest!" Roger objected.

"I wanted you to give our son some advice."

Roger cleared his throat. "Listen to your mom, Lex. Do whatever she says if I'm not around. Don't get all your learning from books. Get out there and do stuff until you get it right. Use what you learn to stay alive and make the world a better place."

Roger fumbled for some way to wrap his remarks. "Do the right thing when you can."

"Nicely done," mom cheered. "We'll edit this later."

Roger was embarrassed. "Are you happy now?"

Mom giggled. "More than you want me to be!"

* * *

The screen went black. Lex looked at Alex with a pained expression. "When was this made?"

Alex came a little closer. "They shot this just before heading out. It was the last time I saw them."

"What were they supposed to do?"

Alex sat on the end of Lex's bed to hide his edginess. "They were supposed to find an old scientist. Somebody with obscure knowledge. Roger's last radio transmission indicated that they'd located him."

Lex turned off the tablet. "Dad seemed kinda goofy."

"He was."

Lex thought about that. "Why did they bring me?"

Alex tilted his head. "Your mom was an only child. She lost her parents at a young age and spent some time in an orphanage. I think she was afraid of losing you."

"Why don't I remember that?"

Alex got up and rummaged through his pockets. "Here. Let me show you this. A lot of us take pictures. It's a way to hold onto our past."

He held up a small, thin digital camera, showing Lex several expanded holographic projections. Lex's Mom and Dad sprang into view, grinning and covered in sloppy mud. Both of them wore faded static camouflage castoffs and running shoes. Body armor and automatic weapons made them look fierce. They appeared to be relaxing on a cracked cement staircase. A spotlessly clean baby wrapped in a blue blanket slouched between them.

Alex flicked through three more similar images. "Here they are in a baby food factory. Here's your dad trading for diapers."

Lex laughed until he cried. "Stop, I'm gonna choke!"

"There *is* more."

Lex wiped his streaming eyes. "I want copies!"

Alex gladly put his camera back into his pocket. "They are already on your tablet."

Lex held the tablet close. "This is mine?"

"Yours to keep," Alex assured.

Lex looked over his shoulder. The reflex was ingrained after years of mistrust. Giving for the sake of compassion was one thing he understood. This felt like something else.

"I am *not* going to school," he warned.

"Don't be so quick to say no."

"Decided and done!" Lex grunted.

# CHAPTER TWENTY-ONE

Lex was led out of the sterile unit, past a trio of uniformed nurses. "Thank you," he remembered to say.

The appearance of a medical robot surprised him.

"Bots!" he shouted while trying to turn back.

Alex grabbed his arm. "It's one of ours!"

Lex halted in midstride. The nurses were laughing.

"*Yours*?" he gasped.

The idea seemed ridiculous, until he saw the nurses laughing at him. Nobody would be that careless around robots, unless…

He turned back to recover his wits and face his fear. The tall, upright machine moved on four small wheels. Its headless white body was covered in segmented panels adorned with medical symbols. Four long swivel arms hung in neutral positions at its sides.

The med bot stopped six feet from Lex, and spoke. "Good afternoon, new arrival. I didn't mean to scare you. Is there anything I can do to relieve your stress?"

Lex adjusted his glasses. "It sounds like a person."

Alex nudged Lex playfully. "Look around, will you? He's not armed. Neither am I. What does that tell you?"

"One of you is very stupid."

"You must be a new arrival," the med bot concluded with a very human male voice.

Lex took a reluctant step closer, ready to make a fist. "What's your job?"

Med bot raised one arm mildly. "Medical assistant, series two, at your service. You may call me Nurse or Helper, if that suits you. I'm not a doctor. Please don't be afraid of me. I am harmless."

Lex took a step back. "You let this work on people?"

"All the time," Alex clarified. He laid a hand over his own heart. "I swear to you, every machine in this complex is friendly to humans."

Lex boldly grabbed one of the med bot's hands, examining its five fingers. Travelers were always telling stories about friendly bots. "You really like people?"

"Humans are my best customers," the unit joked.

Lex released his grip. "Sorry for the interruption."

The med bot reached out casually with one spindly hand to pat Lex reassuringly. "That's really quite all right. Thank you for not harming me. I'll be on my way."

Lex watched it go before turning back to his uncle. "How many machines you got around here?"

"Can't say," Alex hedged while an overhead camera looked down at him. "For safety reasons, we just don't talk about things like that in public places."

Lex eyed the nosy camera. "I'm really starting to dislike those cameras. Like that one. Right there!"

Alex took his nephew by the hand, leading him down a hallway, into a bright lobby. Lex marveled at the vast number of empty seats. "What is it with you people and so many chairs? Are we underground?"

Alex went to a shielded desk to speak with the guard behind a bulletproof barrier. "Yes, we are underground. How did you guess that?"

Lex inspected the man behind the glass carefully. "Seems like everywhere I go these days, there's a lot of open space filled with chairs."

"There were a lot more people," Alex mentioned.

Lex barely heard what his uncle said. He was distracted by a sign over the protected service counter that read: *Airlock 06, Secured Access.*

"Airlock?" he queried while pointing at a blast door on the far side of the room.

"Slow down!" Alex cautioned, "You'll see more of this place, soon enough."

"How do I fit in when I can't ask questions?"

Alex sighed. Most of this installation's population was descended from pre-Collapse professional groups that had been gathered together and brought to this place. Many aspects of "civilized" society remained in practice. Lex wasn't the first who reacted negatively to what must have felt like too many restrictions.

He handed Lex an ID card. "Take this and put it on. Don't ever be without it. That'll get you food, meds, and all sorts of other things."

The teenager took his card, holding it up to the light. A small, shiny, metal clip dangled between his fingers. *Visitor* was stamped into the plastic above his picture.

Lex guffawed at his photo. "Look at that!"

Alex gestured. "C'mon. Let's go. Just follow me. See that mag strip on the back? Don't tamper with it."

Lex giggled. "I used to collect these. The mag strips don't always work."

Alex took the card from his impertinent nephew and pinned it on him. "Trust me, this one works!"

"How long do they last?"

Alex couldn't resist looking down at his own chest. "I really don't know."

"That's lame."

Alex shook his head. "Don't argue with what works. They went low-tech for some things. It's kinda funny, but the most sophisticated machines hated these things."

The idea of cutting-edge machines disliking anything made Lex laugh.

"Shut up and walk," Alex muttered.

Lex followed his uncle out of the waiting area into a brightly lit corridor. Walls cluttered with artwork and security notices made Lex blink. Dozens of people dressed formally walked by without looking at him.

"Who are all these people?" he marveled.

"Think of them as local folks," Alex suggested.

The anonymity was strange to Lex. He was used to being ignored. This inattention made him feel insecure.

Alex indicated a left turn. They walked past several closed blast doors.

"Hard core," Lex appreciated. "Can this place take being nuked?"

"Yes, but only just a little."

Lex chose to be silent as they were processed through a security checkpoint.

Alex pointed to what looked like a subway terminal. "Over there. It's a small, indoor train. We'll ride it back to our housing cluster."

Lex took note of nearby guards and their equipment as they passed. "Must be lots of checkpoints."

"Lots."

Lex looked at the men and women who stood in line for the train. "No stink."

Alex leaned closer. "How often do you bathe?"

Lex took another look at the various people nearby. "Do you guys have enough water for that sort of thing?"

"Yes."

Lex resumed his examination of the people in line ahead of him with new interest. All of them were adults in their mid-twenties or early thirties. They dressed formally, like others he'd seen. The scent of perfumes filled the air. "Some of these people are *fat*."

A pudgy, red-faced man turned to face Lex. "Please keep your thoughts to yourself!"

Lex wasn't sure how to react. He watched his uncle.

Alex smirked and shook his head, *leave him alone*.

"I'm new around here," Lex explained.

"I can see that." The overweight man turned away.

"Easy…" Alex warned.

Lex straightened, possessively gripping his tablet. "I've seen fat people in movies. Never met one."

The insulted man turned back to confront Alex. "With all due respect, sir, please tell him to shut up. I've had a long day. I don't need this!"

Alex put a firm hand on Lex's shoulder when he started to move. "Citizen, I really am sorry about this. My nephew is a bit high strung. It's his first day inside, and he's not –"

"Don't make excuses for me!" Lex interjected.

"Somebody needs to," the outraged man sneered.

Lex bristled when the people around him laughed. "D'you want a shot at me?"

"How rude!" the man protested while turning away. "I'm going to take the next train."

Lex tried to make some sense of the strange moment. He would have never let that kind of insult go in the enclave. Others talked. Backing down would hurt his reputation.

His uncle and the people around him showed disgust. None of them appeared to have any interest in a fight.

"Good," Alex commented after the incensed man was gone. The train arrived, filling to capacity very fast. Lex strained his neck trying to look in every direction. He sat next to Alex.

The train began to move swiftly. "I think I figured this out. These people are all unarmed. They don't mess with each other. Is that normal?"

Alex wilted under a sudden barrage of angry stares from the people around him. "We do things differently. No, we don't mess with each other. That's a rule."

Lex folded his arms and sat quietly as the train sped through a dimly lit tunnel. "I get the impression that Haven has a lot of rules. Is that right?"

Alex rapped his bare knuckles on a clear window. "This whole thing is what they used to call a fallback. Fancy way of saying it's a bunker for what's left of the government to hide in until they get their act together."

"That would explain why there are so many rules."

Alex glared at somebody behind Lex who was eavesdropping. "Yes, Lex. There are a lot of rules here. Keeping the peace means that all of us have limits. Learn 'em and live with 'em, or you will get tossed out! Nobody is immune, not even me."

The young man exhaled, trying to control his anger. "It feels like I've spent my entire life trying to get here. None of what I see comes close to what I imagined. I am grateful, don't get me wrong. Feels like I don't belong here. I know that makes me sound like a jerk –"

"You're fine," Alex interrupted.

"No, I'm not!"

Alex pointed at the nearest door as the train slowed. "This is our stop. Trust me, Lex. Everyone who comes from the outside gets twitchy. Six months from now, you won't want to leave. All of us will be laughing about how much of a pain in the butt you were."

The train came to a full stop. Lex stood and got off with his uncle. They walked across a long, wide platform to the exit. A military robot stood guard near the door.

Lex stood in front of the machine. He admired its olive drab surface. Arms, legs, and cranial turret gave it a humanoid appearance. Markings all over the body identified gun ports and access panels.

"I have never seen one of these in such good shape," he pointed enthusiastically. "Is this thing on?"

"Online," the bot announced with a synthetic voice.

Alex calmly pulled his nephew away from the robot, dragging him through the crowd. They passed through a secured check point on their way to a shiny escalator.

"Don't talk to the hardware," he scolded.

"Do they have a bad attitude, or what?"

Alex stood behind his rowdy relation, herding him upstairs into a busy concourse. "That bot is going to report his encounter with you."

"So?"

Alex was fed up. "Okay. Tomorrow, you're going in for official orientation. They'll explain all of this to you. Don't say another word to anyone or anything until we get back to my apartment!"

Lex bit down on his anger and followed Alex through an indoor garden and up two wide flights of rolling stairs. They stopped in front of a large door.

Lex peered up at the artificial sky, then down at the lush arboretum below. Sound of fast-running water reached his ears.

"Indoor forest?"

Alex put his hand on a palm reader. It chimed before opening the door. "Are you ready for this?"

Lex adjusted his glasses and fumbled with his shirt. "I don't meet a lot of people who are happy to see me. What should I say?"

"Start with 'hello,' and don't steal anything."

Lex felt his stomach flutter as Alex pushed the door open wider.

A dozen voices cheered when anxious eyes caught sight of him.

He looked furtively at his uncle. "What if they don't like me?" he fretted

Alex waved at the people inside. "Don't be so quick to think the worst about us. Give us a little time and we'll answer all your questions."

"He's here!" a woman shouted warmly.

Alex continued to hold the door open with one hand. "Welcome home, Lex. There's no way for us to change the past. All we can do is help you make a better future."

Lex took a deep breath and plunged in.

# EPILOGUE

Tennyson stopped near the front gates of Lakewood. Midmorning sun in a blue sky warmed his body, reducing various aches and pains. Decades of life underground would have made it difficult for any human to tolerate so much bright light or walk long distances. He did it easily, despite his age and declining health.

Tennyson's getaway from the nuclear explosion hadn't been quite fast enough. He'd been caught in the outer edge of the electromagnetic pulse. It had damaged him in a way that could no longer be repaired. "Always did know it might come to that."

This fortified enclave seemed to be quite promising. Men and women who passed through his subway station thought well of the place. They made it sound like these people worked hard to build a better future.

As far as he could determine, they were mostly salvagers who wanted a home. The rest were down on their luck, looking for work that would get them food and shelter. As per human norms, some crime was inevitable.

The old android adjusted his load, moving his pack over one shoulder. His pump shotgun was under wraps to avoid provoking the sentries he was about to address. "Very good, then. Let's see how friendly you are."

Unbuttoning his long, brown, leather trench coat allowed anyone who cared to see that he wasn't carrying any handguns. One less things for greedy guards to take. The wide-brimmed, brown, leather hat Lex had given him felt good on his white-haired head. A knotted wooden cane completed the image he wanted others to see.

"Hello at the gate!" he greeted from yards away.

Two muscular men wore body armor while sitting behind a sandbagged machine gun. The timbers of a massive pair of wood gates overshadowed them.

"Looking for a handout?" one of them challenged.

Tennyson stood motionless at a respectful distance. "No handouts, thank you. I'm here to see about a job."

"What are you good at?" the senior sentry asked.

Tennyson pointed south, in the opposite direction he'd come from. "I was wondering if you need somebody to look after your orphans."

The suspicious soldier bobbed his crewcut head. "We got orphans. Too many of them, if you ask me. What makes you right for that kind of job?"

Tennyson struck a pose, both hands on his cane. "Life has taught me to appreciate the value of children who've lost their parents. A little compassion and some discipline can make them grow up to be good citizens."

"Citizens?" the second guard queried his comrade.

"People," Tennyson interjected quickly.

"Have you done this before?" the lead man asked.

Tennyson bowed in a common show of humility. "I've dealt with every kind of person you can imagine."

"Still doesn't explain why you want that job."

The dying construct thoughtfully scratched his beard. "I don't have much time left."

"We can see that by looking at you," the inquisitive veteran quipped.

Tennyson focused his full attention on the skeptic. "All I can do is ask for a chance to do something positive in the time I have left. I can do the job with very little. Please, ask your leaders. I'm sure we can make a deal."

"You sound educated," the attentive man observed.

"I am," Tennyson acknowledged.

The taciturn guard argued briefly with his comrade. Tennyson watched with veiled interest. One of them was open-minded, the other was not. The junior sentry was shouted down after a few seconds of swearing.

"Stay right where you are," the insightful soldier demanded. "We'll send somebody to see about you."

"Thank you," Tennyson replied cordially.

A messenger was called for. The second man seemed to reevaluate the new arrival. "What's your name?"

Tennyson touched his hat, thinking of Lex. "Call me Preacher."

# INDEX

# ABOUT THE AUTHOR

Justin Oldham is a legally blind writer who lives in Anchorage, Alaska. He holds bachelor's degrees in political science and history. He is the lead developer of *A.C.: AFTER COLLAPSE®*.

Unrelated works in the science fiction genre include: *The Fisk Conspiracy, Tales from the Kodiak Starport*, *Bibix*, and *Crisis at the Kodiak Starport*. His nonfiction works include: *Being Legally Blind: Observations for Parents of Visually Impaired Children, Living with Low Vision*, and *Your Ocular Prosthetic*.

A long-time Alaskan resident, Justin's many interests include collecting books related to the Cold War. Reading, writing, playing strategy games, and home improvement projects keep him busy.

For more information, visit his website at http://www.justinoldham.com. For more details about any of Justin's many books, please visit our website at http://www.shadowfusionbooks.com.

www.ingramcontent.com/pod-product-compliance
Lightning Source LLC
Chambersburg PA
CBHW070615310726
48982CB00001B/88

* 9 7 8 1 9 3 5 9 6 4 6 6 7 *